Deeply Privileged

New Work for the Mortal Empire

Wayne E Ludvickson

Cover illustration © 2006 Studio SFO

Produced by Studio SFO 3145 Geary #713 San Francisco CA 94118

Manufactured in the United States of America.

Ludvickson, Wayne E., 2006

Deeply Privileged.

ISBN 978-0-6151-4360-6

The Minutes

I

It was the middle of a long summer night. I was standing in a valley made of dirty sand. Dead dry vineyards covered its faraway slope reaching up, supplicating the void; rows of wizened dwarfs slowly blowing away in the dust of Time. Fossils scattered under the clouds. In darkness, stillness, oppressive heat, interminable heat. Without even the slow waltz of a solitary cricket playing below the inky stars.

That's when you see them, as I did from another angle. The pair strangely brighter, arcing with dangerous speed over the murky firmament of the world. You might hear their speech together too, in the silence of those neglected fields just outside the immense Dome of our Megalopolis—and many secrets would be revealed to you on that night. There are secrets for which war is too small a word! You want to call to them with every art you know, as I did from every angle, but they're too distant.

Come outside of your Dome now, just a little bit. Take a fistful of sand. Stand in the expanding desert of our world. Who can catch up with it? Write them a letter in the dust.

On the planet of our origin there was an old proverb, haven't you heard it? *Love and hate are two horns on the same goat.*

We have hitched our wagon to a falling star. It burns so brightly our eyes are glazed with magnetic ions. Like frozen ash in the ruins of Pompeii, the ones who will stare that way forever, deeply into each other's eyes. Our fate is incontrovertible, and it is evidenced. You will read on this book until its end. Plummeting contemplation already submerged in a flood of new experiences. You can't help but allow it to flow into a new Mississippi, a Mekong mother-of-waters that will nourish the millions of your yet undreamed-of souls.

An incontrovertible fate. You'll have to admit you're pulled by this plunging steed before you can anticipate my increasing speed. Our nature must be recognized—the horizontal fall, the majestic stars ascending, the coming splash of repercussive inferno such as that which extinguished the primitive reptilian rulers of our planet and drove their cunning descendents into caves to evolve like men for a short time. Prepare yourself for this new life, steel your grip. You aren't the first nor the last who's seen the glassine atmosphere of your planet penetrated! Knowledge of events criss-crossing together in sub-atomic foam. Who wouldn't be interested? These fragrant pages of deep milk churn as you burning grasp the horns of your doomed steed. And while the descending sunset looks merely an ecstatic slaughterhouse to most mortals, you already sense the nourishment of a secret life. It is evidenced.

III

We rode on. We were twelve. The greased clatter of our proud chariots' TransmuFormed vehicle was a small van, we sat cramped, and no one was satisfied with the forms. Our bodies were too rough, in the face and the fingers, not quite human. The Spectrum discipline TransmuCasts us into a certain world in a certain time, for which it selects a range of appropriate sentient forms. Obviously it hasn't been perfected at this juncture. Maybe I will have more space to explain its operation later on, but that is not the subject of this book, as you know.

I look out the window of the van, moving my creaking neck, at the rushing world. Two dogs, a gold and a black, play wrestling in a lush field overlooking the sea. I looked again at my companions sitting uncomfortably in dysfunctional bodies, especially the one female in the front whom the rest stared at greedily. These biologies were irresistible, could they be used at all for our purposes without a gangbang or a cannibalism? We all felt the same frustration, thought becoming more difficult, less lucid. The whole scene, the feelings, total sensation was crushed out just as you crumble a sheet of paper in your fist. Blossom extinguished.

'Why can't we enter this world in our original forms?'

'Why don't we enter with yours?'

'I would be all things to all women.'

'I could change a masterpiece ...'

'Bigger arm ...'

'Lust for life!'

'You are losing control of the mission ...'

Why, why, why. The voices came from the complete darkness of our caucus. What is distance in such darkness? It remains dark so the participants would not recognize each other elsewhere. We therefore meet at certain times destined by our predecessors. These may be revealed to you. We used a nom de guerre ... But you are still failing. You are a long ways from recovery. Be prepared to turn many more pages yet because you have raised your life in several glass cages kept continuously before your mind's eye, and they are just starting to burst from within.

'You are losing control of the mission. We must not do this ... This secretude between us, this tacit wall, invisible sheet—its purpose is spent. Distance, obscurity, obfuscation, the old discipline is deflecting us with pointless eloquence, all nonsense. We don't know who we're talking to or who we are or what we're going to do! Fancy whispering. Its use has become a hindrance.... Come out! Emerge with your faces. Ride up here now, dismount silently at the appropriate pause and approach exactly as our long camaraderie allows and demonstrates. Your great steeds will continue their orbits without you a while. Emerge from black shadow, from the agreed secrecy we share away from the Enemy. The Enemy's weak minions are ever so numerous near this low level that concerns us. Their weakness conceals terrific malice, none of you could measure it. But the Enemy cannot approach us if we show strong together. It is time for trust between us as ourselves. Take off your traditional mask. Krystal Elioud, Bloom, Captain Rice, Duchess of Milk, you others, You-Whose-Name-I-Don't-Know, press through the distance now. Space like a thin papery sheet only separates us at all. Press in and participate, yes, we are as one. So one by one emerge from stations shrouded throughout the Cosmos ...'

The major called us and waved us in. His own head the first to emerge, slightly balding, came comely and rectangular, hair cropped short; moustache iron grey; pale eyes keen as the hunter's though warm; body fit, strong necked. Eyes insistent and patient. One felt like standing to attention before him, whether concerned with protocol or not, out of respect for the generous gallantry which emanated from his whole person. Each of us was filled with similar surprise and admiration finally meeting the faces of those whose strange names we had known and worked with for a long while.

'To love and not to be destroyed by it,' he intoned the prime object of our investigation as we all arrived—we knew it well.

'But we can't even form up decent bodies in the plane of love's growth anymore—on the planet of passion's most complex manifestations--call it low if you like, Major!' Krystal's sweet voice protested, her long silver gown seen like a boat in the night as she sprung slowly from an unseen carriage.

'Perhaps the *weak* operations of the Enemy perceive and frustrate our important Device,' spoke He-Whose-Name-I-Don't–Know with a hawklike glance at me, whom he knew.

'Only where discouragement is sewn, where morale weakens, where doubt dissolves mind's striving for truth.' The major continued to wave us in. 'Remember inspiring examples of determination from Earth's history!'

'I do remember.' agreed Lieutenant Nester Cone. He was from a long line of Ranger families, young, tall, respected. I thought he was kind of too dour. 'Where even Watchers were not immune to excessive pride as they stood on the flat rock above the waterfall—but it wasn't water—white and foamy still! Quickly making their lascivious oath.'

'We are the Vigilants now, Nester. We must all be wary with this subject,' the major suggested. 'Evil is cunning but stupid; Goodness is not boastful, therefore capable of vast intelligence ...'

'To get intercourse with the beautiful children—' Nester went on.

'We *know* the story,' Krystal warned in surprising agony, but Nester finished as he always did.

'Remember how desperately their chief stood above the waterfall with his hands in the void, bringing planets into being. The first you recall was colored as the void: he could grasp it but not enjoy it, and it smelled of dog. The second was huge and of more fire than a sun as it rolled forth. Horses and men fell within its horizon tumbling as it did. Samyasa was sorry for his seductions, so his worlds didn't substantiate.'

'Such a name! They desired a mortal empire on Earth, Major Bunder ...?' Bloom from Flower Haven rotated and we heard.

'It is the very sphere of passion's hottest crucible,' the Major answered, unsurprised at the astonishing form of an Alien Advisor. 'Universally envied and unenvied, hated and loved. Something peculiar in its situation or composition. Where profanations are transcended endlessly and the universe nourishes its own roots. Moving spectacle! Not only in the ancient era, but beyond these obscure ages when the humans contested in total war with the Enemy's weak minions who had taken on reptilian forms in hordes of single-minded vicious infantry. I shudder, but training doesn't permit fear in sound of gaping whelps, barks, and hisses.'

'Oh, must we return there? through all that again?' the Council complained together.

'But their emotions are so talented,' the sarcasm-dripping honeyed voice of He-Whose-Name-I-Don't-Know wove through shadow. 'The salty spread open sea, the tang of longing; the gaping bitterness of nostalgia underneath an embracing nightsky filled with stars … It seems those humans are defined by what destroys them.'

'The survival of love is our mission!' Krystal snapped.

'Ours *is* a mission to love,' the massive Duchess of Milk interposed to soothe warmly. 'But we must survive, somehow.'

'Did we miss something in our previous incarnations which is now prohibiting this Council from gaining a foothold on the present planet?' Major Bunder asked everyone.

'We can't find the right forms for that world at this time …' Krystal repeated, her face in soft anguish.

The problem had something to do with me, and I desired to soothe her even lovely frustration. In those days I did not realize how deep it ran.

'Krystal, Council, all of us … There are myriad universes occurring spontaneously. Manifestations of every possibility. The infinite totality is called Multiverse. We who are withdrawn, we who re-enter and assist, we are therefore 100% capable. Yes, there is an obstacle to my Device, some force of resistance on the planet which hitherto was not present. Let us recall, if you will, my previous penetrations; they were not disappointing. I speak of the human world, since that is my origin, as it is some of yours,' I glanced irresistibly at Krystal, who incidentally is not as me, actually, but her story not now. 'Our world has been created and recreated many times. I saw humans themselves unlock destruction with an amazing technology, TransmuDream, which self-indulgence perverted. The ability to make every fantasy manifest immediate with displaced matter caused the implosion of large quadrants of the Multiverse. Nature could not sustain such abuse. And human persons were crushed by the obscenities of virtual freedom. Point out to you the human mind's lust for witnessing total repetitive annihilation—

War is too small a word for what repeated. I survived this and received my first commission. I attended the burying of the cube-shaped athanors of that accursed Device in a hidden pattern on my planet. Even so, I was fated to see our reborn world protect itself against similar fates in vain. Yes, it was too late to take such toys away from those grown so accustomed to them. Earth had long become a plaything of its egoistic gods. The masses who were left naked and power-famished without their machine, unable to sustain themselves without it. We began to nurse the species, we who could, Cosmic Rangers born like me to survive forms and chaos in biologically essential realms discovered with that same technology. We who re-enter and assist. We were few assigned to it, the 7th Legion. I was low among them. But humanity sold its crushing freedom yet again when those ancient exiled beings whom I must name, the Fallen Watchers who still haunted the labyrinthine caves below a shrunken surface, emerged from the brown cracked earth with the impudent wishes of our desperate species.'

'They were still there?' Krystal Elioud started, but was silenced by a longside glance from the major. I did not understand this exchange.

'TransmuDream had opened the universe. In hotpink delights not forgotten by the living. We who had fantasized longingly for a new art to give back those godlike powers lost. Instead we were thrown the scraps of a pornographic infinity in which our new masters dwelt constantly. A few crumbs of regulated pixilated orgy meant much to a stagnant groping people. A computer became useless for anything else. Humans were willing slaves to an empire that sucked the life from their weakened captives until it was blind drunk with human souls. As if our history describes the digestive tract of spiritual beings. An obese Beatrix with a Fallen Name dominated every essential biological function greedily and indulgently. Expanding grossly until living nature began to vomit from countless pores in mineral orgasm. Another edifying self-destruction unleashed, which it was mine to monitor not to praise. Over-indulgence on a grand scale of universal nerves. Imploding neon voluptuousities, swollen hotpink membranes blown in collapsing fluids. Soft cave-ins of unutterable intimacy across ashamed worlds. I escaped their livid irruption and fled in the teardrop spray of minds released ...'

I paused then, forgive me, remembering the companions of my own world perished in unswervable weakness.

'I returned to this Council and was promoted, by the kind attention of our masters. We who have withdrawn and re-enter. I was placed in charge of regulating appropriate forms for our Scout operations, because of my long experience in and out of a sub-dimensional membrane. This has proven one of my happiest times. The success of our various incarnated configurations is ecstasy, but not complete. Although we have rescued a good number of heroes from their various universes during catastrophes like the ones I've just mentioned which occurred to my own home, others we have not. Although we have assisted lonely survivors through ordeals of mineral implosion, through the loose despair of scattered warmth, through loneliness in a station inaccessible to common fellowship—we still have work to do. Forgive me, Major Bunder, if I detail hurriedly the obstacle of our present operation.'

'Proceed, Captain.'

'Thank you. Scenario review: it is Earth after TransmuDream, and its second reordering. If you recall Earth, you will recall with whatever humor the birthplace of that technology which allowed humans to manifest any reality imaginable—using fluidly displaced matter and elements from other related zones of its universe. As my species craves pleasure and more undisciplined bodies indulged in physical fantasy, an increasing amount of outer space was subverted. Finally—one cannot boast because it is shameful—there were excited ideas among my people for which there is no word enough. Nature collapsed. Her laws rotten and beyond her. We know the results on the inside. Every one of you had received an issue of the TransmuCast report I sent escaping from the Event at the time ...

'Restore your minds now to our present operation: codename Deeply Privileged. There is little difference between before and after, at least less than expected with our old Gelatinous Cubes hidden in a secret pattern around the globe. Yes, we hid those indestructible conductors of the TransmuDream technology, and were right to do so. With the apocalyptic fall of those lower gods who ruled at the close of its pornographic infinity, there was no one left there deemed trustworthy of such a charge. I refer you to the proper archives. And yet the survivors of my species, being what they are, were ever eager for their autonomy. We were begged to consolidate the remaining resources of that exhausted sphere under another vast shelter, and thus life goes on in protective Domes over the human populace once again. Due to the recent elemental drain and insufficiency, technological progress has stagnated beneath a limpid Dome. The Megalopolis resembles a transparent cage of decreasing cares and increasing oblivion, naked upon the shores of my planet's radioactive wasteland; everything is sold for a self-absorbed undeviating pattern of sad defensive staidness. Its culture circling around and around the memory of catastrophe. Transfixing themselves with self-pity's violent fantasies of futile revenge and regret. There is no deviation, no nourishment, no reflection adequate to repairing this disastrous wound, no strength to exercise the broken bones of my species. There is no poetry. There are trapped souls. It is an exhausted place that we have tried three times to enter unsuccessfully, without achieving a definite fix on proper form. Is this clear to you? It has not been our habitual mode, has it? There is some obstacle in that Quadrant attempting to deny us our routine investigation of an imploded world. There is some sick interest at work profiting from the isolation of a historical submission—'

'Steady, Rice. Don't get carried away by conspiracy ...'

'Pardon me, sir. But I have seen interior conspiracy and I know its smell. I realize that there is still the minute possibility of mere inertia, or even a collective resistance of consciousness after not too distant trauma. Our charges want to be left alone. They don't want intrusion. Even were there a festering atrocity just below the surface, which our patrol could neutralize—'

I was again interrupted, but by He-Whose-Name-I-Don't-Know. His dark eyes poked over me continuously.

'That kind of resistance is normal in these depressed cases, Captain Rice. It simply has a tendency to continue too long. Self-protection becomes fossilized in a regime involving very little sensory input or variety of imagination while the bodies themselves struggle to flow naturally. It is the ape of societal peace, and has led to those Events for which war is too small a word. And yet your Device does not allow us to investigate this example, on the planet of your own origin—' a momentary sinister pause, 'Captain. I do not suspect you, but I want to know what you suspect.'

There was some commotion among the Council. The blackness alternately froze and blazed with iridescent light. To me, the alien bodies of several became more visible in instances I will not soon forget.

The Major quieted us with a word and beckoned me to go on. I have a distinct feeling that he knew what I was going to suggest, and that I felt bound to do it. He watched me with his wide open pale-colored eyes, keen and soft, pitying and proud.

'I should become Deeply Privileged. I will enter alone. There is still enough energy in the Device to engineer one human body, male, certain number of chromosomes. He must be born from woman. He must live in knowledge and ignorance as best he can. He must acquire our mission through circumstance and intuition. A life, in fact ...'

There was an uneasy silence. No one approved of the idea, but no one saw another alternative. The obstacle had to be investigated. It was *my* planet. But the chance of failure, of memory loss, of indirection, even subversion was a margin unknown though admittedly very wide.

'Renegades have been known in that Quadrant, haven't they, Rice?'

'What are their names, Rice?'

'Where are they from?'

'How would a child fight a Renegade?'

'An ignorant child?'

'How could you recognize the Enemy or his minions?'

'Rice, you haven't answered my question. Are the TransmuDream Cubes still hidden safely?' He-Whose-Name-I-Don't-Know's dark-lidded sanguine eyes bored into me like a slow sword, challenging, flicking at my motionless face.

'There will be enough energy for two.' Major Bunder's firmly reasonable voice filled the DreamCouncil chamber. 'One human male to be born and one female. Krystal Elioud, an appropriate choice descended from an old family of that unfortunate planet, renowned for extraordinarily searing beauty, will also go and be born again among that species—if it is not too much to ask of her, Miss Krystal?'

Her emanation tightened visibly at her slender white throat for just a moment. She raised her head elegantly, 'It is not.'

She knew what each of us knew. In our battalion of Ranger Scouts loyalty to Major Bunder was unquestionable. We gave it to him willingly in the face of any apprehension, whether for ourselves or the others whom we did not or could not even know. I do not exaggerate if I say he knew us all. I have seen few commanders, human or spirit, able to meld so cleanly the elite of various sentients into such an instrument as we.

IV

To live in the Domes ... It is not the business of this book to record my personal doubts ... but to live an entire unprotected life in the protecting Domes ... Our human crimes have left a stinking trail throughout history, so winding long and iridescent, so indecent it could be followed by a puppy. An old dog finds it very easy. An ostrich sniffs it out. The vegetable kingdom is aware. A supermarket teems with it. Your life is pervaded with the scent of this festering wound which you have never cared for. Look upon the Earth and how we have left her since the irresponsible indulgence of a technology in solipsistic revolution. It is a night of stagnation. An evernight in which unguessible formations breed. The night is a deep one: it swallows the conjunction of furniture in this room where you read, your so-called friends, the miniscule activities of your profession. Berserk you still plunge, ricocheting from the shock to your arrogance. Monkeying between ghosts of love and hate while life passes you by. And all you learn is how to repeat your mistake on an ever larger scale. Is there no limit to the crazy imaginations we allow a sour smelling conscience to lead?

There is. Though it lies not entirely in your virtues which are so many that words fail to count them. Poets try with all their lives' adventurous power. A heart with its arteries and veins extending to every living being and aware of the natural beauty in the conjunction of objects. Bravery has led you through these encouraging pages so far. Your pride has not been offended here, since the shroud of rose petals has been thrust away between your open eyes and mortal destiny, to an appropriate station, and you have remained polite and magnanimous, yourself. Let yourself travel.

My entry would be difficult. Riding in and out at full speed, til latching to a motion greater than my power of steering, than my own existence. I spoke with Krystal many times during this period of preparation: we were to be born as twins from the same womb, aiding each other always through the life. Arrival time, destination—these had been planned from existing records, and we merely had to review them like the sum of maps. A fine detail of the technology involved would lend you some warm security, and it wouldn't be as boring as reducing your food to chemical constituents either—you may enjoy it even more when the cause of your appetites is so clear. But the immense difficulty lay seething in our vulnerability. The mind's tools for bending the reality of my being to adapt would return to us in time, in time; words, for instance, would return as the old language was retaught to us, and I would choose those which describe and identify. But for me, it was inconceivable. To enter as a baby, down the unseeing passage of accident, which could be orchestrated just as easily by our Enemy ... A bit of luck was called for by everyone I left behind, not to mention he who took the dive.

Deeply Privileged

[The following is Captain Rice's report on his mission for Deeply Privileged, as it was TransmuCast to us in its entirety, apparently from his earliest relevant memories of the mission. Always the dutiful Cosmic Scout.. I have included his proceeding characteristic minutes of our last Council meeting before that time in order to give an accurate portrait of the Captain's mind and intention before the actions he took which some may find questionable (not because I particularly enjoy his illustration of my face emerging from the underground we then practiced). It seems to have been written to his own people, as he composed all that he had done of value, and intended to be made into the archaic form of a leaf'd book for them. At the same time it is a report to me. Pieces also occur, as you've seen, which must have been addressed to those riding between the worlds.. A strange and purposeful codex indeed. One notices the anachronisms of Earth (perhaps similar to the way in which our division is still referred to as a legion!). One notices the dialects of Earthen speech. Captain Rice since then has been reported missing in action. Read on then, your Excellency, the words of himself in his own home origin and be satisfied to know that I have recommended him in absentee, as his commanding officer, promotion and our Heroic Human Star of the Multiverse commendation. That may surprise you after reading this; we will have to bear in mind what we know of the ultimate nature of his species, your Excellency. It must be noted here that we have received no report to date from Temporary Krystal Elioud. There appears to have been a miscalculation in their respective points of entry. Her dossier and reasons for contract have been submitted in A-14 code: Pleides Arrowhead Taurus (PAT), which had been accepted with honors at the time. Possible causes of noncommunication are as of yet under investigation, including probable references below—Major Arthur Bunder, Cosmic Ranger, 7th Legion]

I

Acel Daniel was born a boy of natural goodness. His tawny and good-looking thin body, hair, small eyes almost too bright for him in any mirror, each of his senses was deep and persistent. This didn't prevent him from miscalculation and ignorance. Like some people, he desired rather to better his skills whenever shown, even painfully, their frustration, their shortcoming. But more than that, as the little years went on, Acel also began to wonder if his own measure of his shortcomings wasn't suffering a shortcoming. And if it was, did this mean that he should expect less or more of his brain?

One afternoon Acel was finished with imagining a great battle alone in his room with his toys. After all, wherever it began would not be resolved in total victory or surrender for either side—Nature is not so fragile. A careful boy, Acel put away these plastic toys and skipped outside under the drooping shaggy myrtles of the front yard. The silent summer afternoon of a world under the Dome. A yellow flower grew there in the shade, from a hoary dandelion patch in the grass. Acel bent and plucked it easily with a tough snapping noise. He raised the multi-petal flower above his face like a small fiery sun and twirled it up there between his fingers, staring at the yellow toothy flames spinning like petals of a small flower he held by the shortened stem.

Something caused him to turn his head. Dark legs were evident first. Then the bodies of Freddy and Guy sauntered over in the silent summer afternoon. Acel sprung up and asked if they'd like to have an adventurous battle with swords and equipment from times of old, he could hook them all up to the TransmuCast in five minutes. But they had other plans in motion. They were going to the Outskirts to play. The end of the Dome wasn't far from where they all lived. There was a lot of excitement from there lately, since entrance/exit had recently been deregulated. Acel was not afraid of the Outskirts, but there was a different and exciting mood there. It was strange. He could not explain his reluctance and watched them walk away in the sun like noble strangers.

It seemed Acel had been sitting surrounded by a very low jungle of grass just a moment when three girls whom he knew appeared. They were walking in the same direction. A broad thin cloud of fume crawled over the crystal shell surface of the vast Dome above. The girls were talking together merrily and Acel remained immobile, anxious, watching them from the shade.

'Radiation can create anything it wants to!' the fairest curliest was explaining. 'Cats and flowers all come out, cats with flowers growing out of their eyes! Birds with velvet skin! And intelligent dragons who breathe pink snow shooting out of their mouths!' Acel knew this loud girl's name was Andrea C.

'It sounds a little frightening, doesn't it? I thought it was just all black. My father went to the Outskirts hunting before, and he said it was all black.' That was Rachel Cruz. She had black long hair like magic silk, as many families in this Area. She was beautiful, and everything about her bewitching as the deepest night, the night Acel once saw a real star twinkling through the incessant cumulous high above the Dome. Her eyes were big pools of black wine glistening. Her voice was slightly hoarse and low and she was small as a jewel. But Acel unfortunately had never yet spoken with her; his agitated mind repelled itself from her fairylike beauty, unexplainably locking his senses, he could only watch her, paralyzed, devour and swallow his body. But then the third girl spoke, which relieved and interested him.

'Snow in the Outskirts while everything's so hot under the Dome? I thought the Dome should make life cooler. Outside, where Nature is sick, maybe Nature has a fever, Nature can sleep sweaty in the dark and have nightmares. So Nature likes us to visit and cheer Nature up! Sometimes I go as far as DreamRidge and make it wet, I pour water under the stalagmites ... They say a Cosmic Ranger slept every night there during the TransmuDream.'

This girl was named Diona, Diona ... he could not think of her last name. She was darkhaired too, and her clear moonlike face became more alluring as lingering Acel concentrated over it, real where the other girl was still unreal.

'Is it all dry there, no seas at all?' Rachel asked her.

'There used to be a lot. But the fish grew legs and walked away.'

'And the dolphins live in Area 6 and men marry them!' Andrea C said. She'd gotten bored of listening. 'There's sharks in the Entertainment Zones that wear make-up and are more beautiful than a sunset. And green coral in gardens! And there's manta rays that fly around the post office like ghosts ...'

Acel stood up because they had come so near and Acel felt it was his honorable duty to do so. With an awkward voice he greeted them through entering their conversation.

'Are there oysters?'

The girls all laughed at him popping from the grass, though perhaps Diona less than the others.

'I am an oyster,' she told him politely.

'Yes ... I'm Acel. What is an oyster's name?'

'My name is Pearl,' Diona told him. Acel liked her face and body because she was lithe and calm and so clearly featured and always smiling slowly. He felt like he could smell her smile like a gentle collision of dawn and sunset.

'That's a weird name!' Andrea C interrupted about Acel's first name. He was slightly embarrassed, though he had heard this before.

'Maybe his name is Every-Grain-of-Sand,' dark Rachel spoke and smiled with a broad motherly warmth.

Diona's and Acel's eyes met again reluctantly and irresistibly.

'Does an oyster try to make a pearl inside?' Acel felt he was explaining the bizarre phenomenon between them. 'If all the oysters didn't try, there wouldn't be any pearls, and the oyster would be spoiled with the sand, wouldn't it?'

'I don't know,' Diona responded. 'But some reaction must happen, for better or worse, if just a tiny grain of sand enters the new oyster ... and only once and forever.'

'The Nature's all crazy at the Outskirts because it was spoiled with too much sugar! Just like a shellfish accident!' Andrea C insisted, obviously bored out of her wits. 'Now there's a big sea of black coffee with dragons in it that snort yellow foam. Some men were hunting one, didn't you hear about it? We're going to go see and visit Nature, like Diona says. Do you want to come, too?'

'Yes,' Acel did want to go, but he didn't want to go with only girls, given they would talk more than play, or play silly, or other people might see him so and think him girlish. 'but I have to finish something at home.'

II

Patient at all odds with himself, having nothing really to do fulfilling his excuse to the girls, finally something came up. Acel's mother was going out shopping, so Acel offered to help.

They took the silver car on the silver roads. The white soundwall slid entrancingly by. Traffic before them shining and hot. His mother seemed awkward at the wheel, although Acel supposed she must've drove often, but he rarely went with her that way. Public transportation under the Domes was cheaper and more carefree.

Acel leaned back and sang popular tunes after the fashion of a certain rural (near the Outskirts) Area, musicians that he'd seen on recorded TransmuCast films at school. They always watched a lot of films at school. No adults had the inspiration to teach intently anymore after TransmuDream. There were hardly any churches either of course, even near the Outskirts on holidays. Acel had never been to one—fanatics, people said. Violently piteous TransmuCasts appealed to the masses instead, and to the lonely for donations. It was almost a joke, but it was like an institution of society, the way things are. Meanwhile the schools promoted social order, naturally, as well as all the technical and economic skills to keep the Domes functioning. However statistics said with evident disappointment that there were always fewer folks around to do the job in the future. In Acel's Area some adults even said parents should just keep their children at home and show them how to cook and hunt what's out there, now that the Homeguard had taken steps to deregulate the Outskirts. A problem was there always seemed to be fewer supplies of certain staple commodities, and prices climbed. But Acel was reckoning that if he sung a popular song of his own Area in that rural style, with some energetic music—his friend Robert Trout played some drums—it could really be a hit.

Outside the supermarket a Homeguardsman was waving his arms. He was conducting traffic. When their car came near he asked what they'd be buying today. They told him: meat substitutes, vegetable substitutes, and tiger's milk (for deserts, Acel informed him). But that was a problem now, the Homeguardsman said. He pointed at a NewsCast for Acel's mother. The huge screen depicted a problem in a faraway Area. Near distant Outskirts. Someone in a tiger farm went haywire and a compromise of authority had led to some confusion, and the large groups of tigers had gotten out and were eating office workers in the street. There was a lurid image of two tigers eating office workers in white uniforms.

'One wonders how God lets our little world go on, eh?' the Homeguardsman snorted sympathetically and waved them on.

'I'm sure the Homeguard will contain this, Mom, Dome Civilization can't tolerate tigers eating office workers in the streets,' with NewsCast-type words young Acel consoled his mother, who was disturbed and frightened by the story ...

A few minutes later Acel followed his mother in beneath the ice-fans. She went on ahead down the narrow aisle of goods, but Acel paused near a table of small ray-umbrellas. They could be useful in the summer sun, when the Dome heated way up there.

He opened one up. It was rectangular in shape, with a golden shell pattern and green fringe. It rotated gracefully emitting a cooling breeze beneath. A dark young man stood before him, bent and peering down at him under the umbrella, thinner than anyone he'd ever seen before in the Dome. His long face did not appear impressed by Acel's investigative demonstration of an umbrella. Acel noticed innocently in his shade that this rectangular umbrella could've been designed to shelter two, and so he began to playfully mutate one of those popular tunes of his Area,

'Two for tea, tea for two

 tea is something I could share with you'

The thin dark young man with curly hair said nothing, frowned, and glanced at the stacked supply of gaudy little umbrellas. Then he said, 'Don't you understand it's bad luck to open an umbrella indoors?'

'Why?'

'Because it means you don't trust the shelter you've come within.' The young man's voice was husky and garbled. His torso leaned back and forth over the table and Acel's umbrella nervously. This made him hard to see. Acel wondered if the man was embarrassed because he enunciated so badly, as if he was a foreigner from a faraway Area, and maybe he was.

'How can anyone open an umbrella beneath the Dome then, and have good luck?' Acel asked.

'That's only the beginning! Who's talking about the Domes?' the mysterious man gruffed out and disappeared.

Acel saw nothing then but the titanium sheen reflecting over the windows, the inscrutable heads, the ears, the whole world he knew under the Dome. Acel felt naked and ridiculous standing there in the middle of the megamarket. Slowly and shamefully he closed the umbrella and put it down. For an instant it entered little Acel's mind that that young man might have been evil … In any event he was inexplicably strange and he gave rise in Acel to a dreadful feeling that he did not soon entirely forget.

III

[The following excerpt came to me included in this position, though I must assume that this account came to him later. We may never know how. However I include it here as well, since Captain Rice did in his report. It is possible we can make more sense of it now than he could at the time.... There are more scenes following from an unknown period or even unknown source as well which I include for your Excellency in the order in which they occurred with the rest of Deeply Privileged—Major Bunder, Cosmic Ranger, 7th Legion]

Dunes of restless dry mud. Purple and brown shifting moist desert, polyp-like sand of a vast rolling field glistening with late dew. Raw'd Nature at her over-stimulated state, perpetual just beyond the sharp ledge of an incomplete Dome. The perpetual yearning dry wound of post-TransmuDream Technology.

This was their time of experience, so that is where they played.

Over the crusty hillocks barefoot flew the three little angels of our previous description. Dark and light and twilit. A cool but humid sultry air locked them in intelligent delirium as they pranced, scattering their artificially grown flower bulbs here and there for Nature's relief.

Andrea C cried out too loudly and leapt down into a shallow gorge, followed instantly and silently by the other two.

'Quiet!' Diona commanded, and closed her hand over the wild curly-blond's mouth. She too had seen Freddy and Guy playing in the silence, bobbing up and down the faint hotpink sky's rippled horizon, and didn't want to be seen—or heard.

'It's fine,' Diona whispered. 'They didn't see us.'

The boys' crude laughter died away. It was a still time. When the girls looked up again together they were numbed with surprise.

A cloaked man stood above them on the dune. His tall form wrapped thoroughly in a hot breeze imposingly and shadowless. No one said anything. Then in an instant movement the stranger hurled his dark brown cloak tumbling away to the sands. He was revealed smiling, young, handsome, blue-eyed and redhaired, in clothing of soft pink and cheerful green, which set the girls clapping with delight.

With a flick of his prince-like head he TransmuFormed into a small rabbit of the same colors—with somehow his same confident silly smile beaming from dark sweet eyes—and the girls cheered louder. The rabbit opened its mouth and ten tiny moons spurted forth, circling the lavender skies in rolling thunder finally exploding a starry orchard of exciting color. Where their living sparks fell to the vivid sands, a pleasant smelling grass spread there, and little deer cavorted to and fro amongst giggling leaves.

'Would you like to play a game?' came a funny and daring voice, as the girls screamed in joyous fear answering automatically, 'Yes! Yes!'

A gorgeous dragon lay before them, scales a long body of mother-of-pearl. Clouds like dream ribs rolled over the sky.

'You may touch me, touch my pleasant and beautiful scales, but gently.' The dragon extended a mobile claw of irresistible gleaming opal.

One by one, the girls manipulated the long exquisite pearly-starry digits.

'Goodness encourages the greatest prosperity and creative freedom. Nevertheless, there is some activity, which gives pleasure but nourishes no goodness. So those manifestations have been called vice. You have heard of these things.'

'Yes,' the girls agreed. 'We've heard of almost everything!'

'These are eruptions which must be balanced with productive order, or they cause abrasion to a soft raw life ... Your lives, three soft delicate little girls, must remain here beyond your Dome with me. You shall stay unchangeably happy here until the hero grows and awakens to find you. Waiting intransigent, beautiful as pink young buds in the earth. You don't understand yet that your heroes will be my heroes. I will open you up to find a living formula that rebels against formula, the harmony of the certain shape of my life. The heroes will be beautiful.'

IV

The TransmuCast News that reported to Dome Area 4 about the three girls' disappearance had come and gone with Humanity's various profound odors of change, in everlasting grief and defeated anticipation. Hope itself changes form, though not painlessly. Life's living grows on.

Acel too grew into a young man. He lived as before with his parents on a middle floor of their blockhouse. But he hadn't spoken with his father for many years, a chubby kindly-looking man with a soft voice, thin yellow hair, spectacles. Acel's father knew that he had helped to raise a conscientious boy after all though, because he himself had always praised the life-sustaining qualities of Dome-life's general maintenance and had chastened his son to resemble such a universal perspective. There had been a time when Acel still received a few significant transmissions from him in this thread. But for years now his dad's body lay immobile while his mind was campaigning far away in a TransmuCast Series with who knows what kind of life realizing his powerful idiosyncrasies, and so has an intermittent role in this report. Perhaps not such an abnormal family in the Dome. As this slow separation became obvious to Acel there began a decade of pained confusion and search, hunger even (to his mother's concern), false stops and false starts. His studies petered out. A fermentation, though without any material gain. This confusion wrongly seemed to him the innate nature of all life for a time, but it was just a despair to which he could not surrender but felt more acutely than others. With unceasing effort Acel reached thirty, the age when a man's brain finally begins to mature and become solid.

At the age of thirty there began in Acel the birth of reason and will, too, in spite of his emotional body. So the man emerges from the boy. The ability to reflect upon the cause of desirable and undesirable stimulation is the prerogative of certain species in the universe, and not very many on Acel's planet, referred to as higher orders by those who appreciate its benefits or are envious of its magic. This had begun to stir and become well alive in Acel's mind, as a baby learns now to walk from object to object, bracing itself between adventurous launches, and lands winding up in his mother's arms. He began to consider self-discipline a good thing with a refreshing taste. That was the way. To emerge from the earlier age of barely mental processes submerged in thick wine of his body's primitive emotion, thinking as sluggishly as one flees in dreams. To act on the deductions of this new art, reason, that was will—and Acel thirsted for more. He was a great seabed filling up with the sea. The experience of volition, like moving his hands for the first time. Opening his mouth at the command of his brain. Awareness of oneself in activity, in existence. A development of the soul, which embraces everything in an undisclosed likeness by specializing raw factors to improve its subject, this is another life-long project that again often falls incomplete in incompetent hands. Just as mature human reason owes its birth to our getting full-grown, thus signaling our awareness of mortality, it must also be properly practiced and exercised to wield anything decisive.

In this increasingly baked stage a wry curl was usually on Acel Daniel's lip. That's how people recalled his face, no matter how long they'd known him. It was because he smiled so easily and was humble enough to get along with almost everyone by now, though was definitely not above sarcasm. Anyone who was ever envious of his charming wit had called him flippant. And yet there were (unknown ever to Acel then) a good many people he'd met in his Area who remembered years later some lighthearted words he'd said in his murmury soft voice and still believed that was how things really were. In fact he was the kind of young man about whom old folks—had there been many around—would've said that there's a boy who has no limit to how far he could go, if he only applied himself and got the proper training. However with reason percolating in Acel's brain there began also his slow retreat from unnecessary human society. No one knew how he was saving himself from the petty squanderings of society. Acel wasn't shy, but this saving preferred compromise and agreement to conflict with others. His manner was strange in the over-compensated unlistening barks that made up most people's conversations on their way between TransmuCasts. He usually joked his way out of situations where he or another might lose face ...

In looks, Acel had grown up longbodied, thinner than most Dome people, not especially muscular but pretty goodlooking in a way between a sylvan nympho or a rustic lunatic, depending on the lighting. His mooncrescent profile was widow-peaked by a patch of sandy uninspired oily hair, which one of his more inspired critics once described as a steak on top of his head. Later he was able to comb it more becoming, if more sinister. There was an obvious taste for pretty women in his movements, especially those of his mouth when he talked with them. Then Acel had as much success as men expected in the Domes--zero. Those large fleshy rumps were just as busy as the men were, and just as eager to get home and turn the world off in a TransmuCast. As Acel grew up he learned to live with it, he did like the others. Though not entirely. Acel wasn't vain, even though he pretended to be sometimes—and he felt, as correctly as any self-confident person, that he could afford the joke on himself for the general pleasure. Occasionally some people got a little raw when he naturally expected anyone else to wield the same budget. Acel was not uncompassionate, apologized too much probably, but his mind was focusing and his circle of acquaintants was narrowing. He was interested in playing tennis casually with a neighborhood friend named Nik in the evenings. They played down at a vacant lot, with a parking chain strung between them for a net. Their manly and generous competition felt an unlimited expression of tactile ungraspable life. Nik was a little older so had an experienced and magnanimous sense of humor. They worked their little jobs and had what little fun they dared in their dull area of the Domes.

But secretly, Acel was more interested in something else. A private pursuit that stirred the bubbling cauldron of his maturing brain's fresh arithmetic. During the many long evenings when the boys didn't play, and Acel's parents were prostrate in their room with the TransmuCast, Acel read books. An activity hardly performed in the universal education! Acel found reading very difficult at first. So many words were so long, and until he found a dictionary he had to presume at meaning from their context. The complex sentences and the way they hung together one after another took years for him to master. He often read the same book over and over many times, painfully sharpening his brain on the cohesion and coherence of its intricate text. The skills required to follow the logic of these pages further set him apart from others. The resulting intelligence, rather than being other worlds offered to him, was actually windows on his own world; multifarious windows dragging his understanding right through them. Reality crumpled under iron blows. A dear pleasure. Those old books were inexpensive but very hard to find— everyone relied on TransmuCast nowadays (just as most men in the Dome did for their experience of sex). But these old books had a sort of different life in their printed words, a distant transmission from a distant friend, in a style of someone else's own making. There were still a very few shops near the Outskirts of the Dome that sold knickknacks, curious gewgaws, described as useless but picturesque junk from the past. However the fad had never really caught on to collect dusty rectangular books. Acel went there sometimes to buy them, and also to forget about the lonely hotpink flashes of beautiful women he'd seen during the past weeks. Already nothing was easy for a mature adolescent, and Acel was already an adult: there was only mindsex in the street anymore. Everyone hurrying home to switch on the TransmuCast of their desire and escape the effort and agony of other people in a stagnating Dome on a deadened planet. But some of the old books talked about interesting times before the TransmuDream implosion, which had left the world how it was today. And once, through months of diligent research, he found one that even mentioned the Cosmic Rangers, who were said to have survived TransmuDream and to still exist somewhere outside the Dome, outside the World, diaphanous and brilliant. Human creatures who could survive the many forms enforced during the catastrophic natural implosion that had defined life as it was now carried out. Indeed the Rangers became like lesser angels, like gods in time. The informal canonization of various remembered personalities as it occurred in some Areas is a subject of the weak religion of the Dome, though too weak to elicit much devotion beside religion's conqueror, the TransmuCast. In fact, the Rangers were known as the original builders of the Dome; the founders of its government; the shepherds of the extant human species, before they left us. This subject had been mentioned, but in no complete way covered in Acel's school. That book, written a long time ago about lover gods in a lower more physically essential realm, seemed to allude to something even personal since reading again and again those strange fiery passages; Acel increasingly desired to go far out there, wherever it was. He became someone profoundly interested in a secret and more essential purpose behind his world, with a secret history, and his brain had already begun to seek ways of deciphering it.

V

The air was stifling, dry. Acel felt no breeze, and yet each time he gazed up to the open Dome-less sky the everpresent clouds had reformed unpredictably thick luminous grey and pink dappled fringes in the aerial sea of continuous thunder. Far away the sun was dozing incandescent behind them, he guessed, immersing the lofty stragglers with wild color as they wheeled to the drums. Across a ditch near him a dried ancient vineyard looked like wizened little creatures calling for a light that had forgotten them.

Acel returned to the anachronistic library in the evening. He had found a job in this little broken-down hole in the wall near the Outskirts that delighted him to no end. 'Mother's Cupboard'—it had to be the only place left like this in the whole world … in Megalopolis. He'd gotten the job through a rare frequency TransmuCast ad, another clerk had hired him; it all felt as anonymous as everything else. It was true that very few people came in, and many of them seemed crazy, and as for the others, Acel felt too shy to utter a word to them. It amazed him that there were others alive that could be interested in these books much, though he readily admitted most of the books were very boring. But anyone who was still interested in reading couldn't be so bad, could they? It was hard to tell. No one was allowed to borrow books out of the library, they were too few, so Acel couldn't always determine how much History the uncrazy ones might be pursuing, the kind of Secret History that had begun to fascinate Acel so much. Only the crazy ones ever left behind any notes, but these were always such fractured portraits, like the primeval scream of some hominid tribe's code of laws. Scraps which might as well be called nonsensical—Acel had even attempted pondering them as well.

Occasionally a burst of laughter would shatter his concentration, but that wasn't so strange, it could happen to anyone. Acel had already realized that much of the worth in a work consisted in this reaction. But usually people just sat. It was cool and quiet, almost easy to think there.

He'd been out of the Dome nine maybe ten hours. His feet itched with sweat. Immediately he found a note on the desk that he shared.

The parchment was rough but smelled as if not long manufactured and not by a machine.

Come out again tomorrow down by the gate. I deem you are of good character. I will meet you there.

The writing is not very neat, Acel thought. A man's, someone who was in a hurry. Or someone who writes so much he doesn't waste time with shapes he knows can be read anyway; or it was written in the dark … Who is it? Is *this man* of good character?

Acel did not sleep perfectly that night. The apartment buildings looked like tall cages from his tiny balcony. Lilting music blew from across the way. And his mind was tuned by questions.

VI

Lavender dustdevils pushed through cracked scarlet earth of a plain at sunset. A small group of what appeared to be ragtag hunters choked and paused in the lonely middle of nowhere. Their worried silence was punctuated by peals of thunder overhead. Glancing at each other, they were harried and sickened with nerves at the peculiar and threatening sight unavoidably hemming and urging them deeper and deeper into desolation since midday. Their leader, a gruff dark man of that thick build which disguises pure heavy muscle, cautioned them to ignore the obscene gigantic lizard that had crawled and scurried hideously on their periphery, circling but edging always closer behind, driving them out ... A mirage, he called it at first, yet led them away from it consistently. It became disturbingly apparent that he, Oxnard, feared this apparition more than any of them. He forbade them shoot at it, he forbade them speak above a whisper or to swear. And now real panic was gathering in.

The other men did not know Oxnard. He came, he said, from an Outskirt far to the north and had invited daringly a bunch of loitering out of work men to go hunting outside, not far from the Dome he said. With bravado some agreed. But eventually it had become apparent that Oxnard had an ulterior plan, too—he was looking for something, something strange, and something far. They asked him no questions however ... A demoniacal word more frightening than an angry Guardsman informed them that questions were not appreciated. As this kowtowed the bravest among them, they all followed like beaten young apes after the alpha male, heads lowered, bodies catatonic with an anxiety of submission.

It had taken miserable impossibly long hours in the dying sun—Carl, the toughest of them (he had once been jailed for spitting on a shopkeeper and following this caper with pummeling a teenage boy) had been nourishing his terrified resentment into profound hatred since being rebuked in such an inhumane (he called it) manner. He'd prepared his tirade, he'd imagined stage by stage the confrontation that fate destined. Sweat poured from his stinking lanky muscular crazy frame, he was delirious with insult and isolation. He would stab big Oxnard as soon as he was called scared. "Who's scared now you're about to die?' he'd sneer as his fist rested against the horrid frantic heart with his buck knife stuck through it. Then they would rush back strategically to their Dome homes, out of this rotten madhouse of weird mutant creations that should be left to die on their own in this useless desert.

He was worrying about the precious moment he would have to open his knife when the attack occurred. A glittering serpent the speed of light. Death enclosed every one of them rapidly with agonizing sudden violence. The heart perhaps stopped during the massacre of a given body before implicitly indicated. The stringy flesh mixed up of skin and muscle wrapped them together bizarrely. With a warm awful smell. 'The lizard!' Carl thought last, but his vestigial ears still heard his evil hero, Oxnard's voice defending against this travesty with a strange despair.

'I know you, you stinking sergeant! You're not so good! You want those Cubes as much as I do. My God, I hate you—I'm free, I'm free, you're not my sergeant anymore, don't you understand, there are no stinking Rangers anymore!'

VII

Acel ate a substantial breakfast which renourished him after the long night. His brain was in a state of discipline such as it had never been before. He looked forward, rather abstractly, to the morning mist that would be clinging over the low dunes of the Outskirts. The eerie light of the Dome had shifted to its faint lime pervasion before the day. Acel dressed sharply, and headed toward the gate.

No one was in the streets at this hour and Acel once more had that piquant religious feeling that he was the last soul alive on Earth. He clung to this feeling, indulged it, nourished it in all the purity and beauty it promised. Acel felt near to God. From his old books impressions of the fanatic ancient religions before TransmuDream came to him, and warmed him with a sense of continuous belonging to the wildly incessant manifestations of our ambitious species. It was all the same this moment as it was then. The mysterious appointment toward which he went, slower than usual, made him tremble with a life's hopes …

Someone important with knowledge and power had noticed his interest in the arcane past, and wanted to learn all about it from him. A beautiful woman, with one shape or another, was so often on his mind. Great amounts of money appeared and burned up in his imagination. A secret exciting life of secret power. A worldwide recognition. The genesis of a vain hyper-dynasty. Or his first thought, that this note could just be from some sick pervert. Acel must be on his guard, there had been awful crimes manifested at the maw-edge of the Dome … but there would still be Homeguardsmen … within seeing … Acel arrived before he could've calmed himself efficiently.

The gate was a vast open mouth where the Dome ceased in a jagged overhang of disused construction. Desolation was beyond. Sleeping silver-garbed Guardsmen leaned about their few wide apart boxes never expecting anything. A small child ran past him with long hair blowing, but Acel felt he must be dreaming because when he glanced back she'd disappeared. A blurring dust spread on the horizon beyond the poisonous Outskirts and slowly blew away to distant cracks of thunder. Some rotting coil of wire to his left seemed a purplish serpent for a mad instant. Acel's early morning lucidity was threatened with terror and he suddenly recalled his job and knew he must take care of many things there before he left into a new life—no, no, it was impossible. A hooded old man squatted casually against a gigantic pylon, and Acel approached him without knowing exactly what else to do.

'Excuse me, sir.'

The man looked up at him. He was younger than Acel expected—surely aged, crow's feet overran the eyes, but the expression was warm, mysterious, playful, grim. One of the most human faces Acel had ever seen, he suddenly thought, yet the most hurried—beneath blue eyes—a painful forced portrait of harried man.

'So you're not as much of a weakling as you look! You, have you ever considered a career in, say, journalism?'

Acel didn't answer. This was who had sent the cryptic message, he understood that.

'You like reading old books, I have seen that effectively. You probably like writing too. That's an anomaly in this place! I can almost respect that. Even though your kind has always been satisfied with being nothing more than an artist of obscure ironies, totally incapable of taking a real life by its horns and leaping into its chariot—in other words, an idiot. I don't suppose a social dropout like you would think much of a career in TransmuCast journalism, would you? You're too sensitive to participate in the world at large, aren't you? To sully your mind with the real efforts of your actual species—its politics, its economic yearnings, its daily fate … You'd like to get away from all that, wouldn't you?'

'I've seen enough propaganda in the TransmuCast,' Acel muttered thinking of his mother and father's addiction, everyone's. Disappointed, he tried to recall if this red face was among those of the crazy who had ever wandered into the library. A face so powerful, confident, intelligent, a rough gravelly voice—why did he sense patheticness? Acel was frightened to think that the same elements of life that were driving this man's eyes to bulge so aggressively also impassioned himself. Did Acel look like that himself to others?

'Which TransmuCast Faction do you represent?' he asked with more suavity hoping to sooth the man's rudeness.

'So you're growing a spine—I almost respect that too! You now, from your readings you must've attained some big picture of the way an individual works for our masters. The one who gathers intelligence, disseminates it to certain channels, and watches it spread through the general public at large. There are different levels of the same practice. Each of these promoting development. A chain of masters and servants. From the significant utterances of a childlike mystic to his only companion, down to the vapid manipulations of a tyrant's paranoid pronouncements which are so historically indicative to someone like me, though there is no one like me. No, you're not like me yet, if you ever could be. Consider it: the message of your life, sent back to those who sent you. What a surprise!'

Acel's long face screwed wry repulsed by the fascinating urgency of this terrible man who had tracked him down. At this point he would've preferred chewing over these weird words in peace, but he was alarmed too.

'How do you know about me?'

'Information is sometimes dear, sometimes cheap. I know something about you, I have watched you. I've invited you to meet me. I do this because you interest me, Acel. I'd like to explain why while we still have time. Let us stroll through the dunes a bit, may we? I love the morning mist.'

Before Acel could decide to react to his caution about this stranger, about whom he also observed was much larger and stronger than he looked while sitting—and was most certainly stranger than he looked anytime—the man rose and they walked quickly out together some while before he spoke again. Or rather Acel followed, deciding it was harmless to appease this dominating personality for a little while. Though it must be said that he was each step by step losing interest. This encounter was not at all like he'd hoped, and there were a few other things he'd rather do on his day off he was sure ...

They walked long past the dried ancient remnants of a dead agriculture Acel had never seen growing in his lifetime. Old remnants of vineyards, an unearthed culvert, so much debris. The shadow of the gaping Dome's Gate fell far behind them. They reached the dunes. The day's heat already starting to weight the air. Trudging and getting down, trudging up and getting down—the stranger was a striding powerhouse of energy. His hood dropped away in an effort revealing mussed thin reddish locks dampening with sweat.

The dunes were cloaked in low swirls of breathtaking fleece. The man's brown cloak fading imperceptible into the colors of the dewless morning's dry earth. The sky became clear in patches as it did so rarely, and the stranger pointed at a shining diamond far above them.

'Look, there! It used to be called Venus. You have seen it before out here. A beautiful name! You may call me that, I think. All my life I have loved that star, have always looked for it and felt more human with it hanging above us all. Would you like to hear some history, Acel?'

Acel stood immobile, breathing heavily with a concoctedly bored expression. 'That sounds effeminate to me, that name,' he tried to ease the heaviness. 'Why not *Sir* Venus?'

The stranger drew back from him slowly as a gorilla, a horrible flush flooding his body and face; thick with spittle, as if he had just received an undeserved sentence, his voice bled with insulted righteousness.

'Have I *ever* said anything so cruel to you yet? Have I *one time* categorized you in a discouraging manner to your face? I don't believe that I have ever dug up your life and tried to destroy you with mockery (though of course I surely could), now have I? *Nyoooooh*,' the word wormed out like a rotten child's. 'Then why do you insist in this bald craving to desecrate my friendly consideration for you so flippantly, Acel? Your little title is just fine for me, I'm sure it's very appropriate as far as you are concerned. My pride can afford all you've got. Now listen to me, *pleeease*.'

Sir Venus (Acel had no other name to refer to him with) sucked in a massive amount of the Outskirt's stale oxygen through two huge red nostrils, ponderously mastering the most violent aspect of himself. The large muscles of his face twitched and his fists clenched. He came very close to Acel who stood on the verge of trembling. He smelled like too much old wine and his tone was bitter.

'I know very well how it's so easy to feel you're extremely special on this Earth. But if only you could realize your folly, boy. Our Masters make us and then cast us out, scorning us for merely following the commands of a nature they designed—for following their example! Is that fair? Where is the conscience that they punish me for a lack of? I had plenty more of it myself far back in your history. It was not so long ago that there were Domes, Acel, much like the one you live in now, Acel, with your squinty eyes so full of little green and hotpink sparks. Yes, a shelter all full of the namby-pamby comforts and niceties that are really the end goal of your people's cravings. Can you believe such a place existed before your present cherished home? Yes, a stale stagnating Dome, so much like yours. Built to shield us from the wasteland caused by erupting advances in technology. Exactly the same people with exactly the same fate in the same structure. An agonizing limitation that imprisons your overpopulating senses—a degenerating Dome, like yours. Built to protect, it now restrains deformingly. No more life could be gathered within it safely. The Megalopolis was strained to an outer tension; civilization had begun to painfully stagnate distended across the globe. At last, forces that are yet indescribable were released into our upper conscious layer of life. Orgiastic feasts of carnal love burst from the very minerals of vast Earth. The Cosmos shuddered as it drew itself around this phenomenon. In our world here it took the form of TransmuDream, an invented technology allowing the manifest of every inner thought immediate! Other beings perceived marvels appropriate to their cosmological abilities. Ah yes, it was a time of which you have read in the first phase of your manhood and study. You are dimly aware of the entire reaction, process of explosion and implosion ... and those who could survive ... In between there was no Megalopolis for a short while, we did without. How so? The jealous gods may have seen it differently, I think ... But now look. Our protective Domes have been built again to shield the masses from the wasteland caused by an erupted advance in technology, everything the indulgence of TransmuDream created and destroyed ... But people are ungrateful, or stupid. It's not so long after that marvelously raped universe, and humanity doesn't have any idea what survived this TransmuDream eruption, and what thrived beyond the space where the lost survivors cringe. They do not know who rides what mounts between the worlds! They do not guess what beings constructed these Domes for them again, when they could not be made free and live.'

There was silence enunciated only by the distant flashes of high lightning. Acel turned and looked up at Sir Venus with a growing awe. He didn't want to take him seriously, or for him to take himself seriously, but he was having trouble thinking up a sarcastic response that wouldn't make him angry again. This was a man he did not want to get on the wrong side of.

'You wear your new sense of respect well,' Sir Venus said with a warm chuckle, a long bead of sweat running down his head, and Acel almost liked him again. Then the large twinkling face immediately took on that unnerving hurried look as before. As if there was a constant struggle going on inside him, between an older kinder man and a younger dangerous and jealous rival who seemed on the verge of permanent triumph.

'And let me remark while we still have a moment that you do possess a secret self and abilities of which you hardly know, Acel. But you would in time, were you ever as brave as me. No, when I came to knowledge I was different than you.' Venus brought his face down close to Acel's again, blue eyes bulging out red, and spat in a flurry of whispers, 'A day will come, it must come soon, when you will instruct *me* … all about how to say things ... secret things. *Where* to say them! There is a secret thing, I am sure, locked within you, within your brainstem! The knowledge of a previous life must be somehow stamped into this body. We must be able to recollect it! Or else all for what these churning births and deaths we are subject to—if we cannot build upon the last? I refuse to be merely the flatulence of an ever-writhing infinity, without purpose nor reason. I know what happens if you just leave everything up to the authorities—nothing! For such ideas have I been exiled, dissections I had petitioned for from the experts—nothing! Do it myself! I too have things to report from exile. Does it take a brain surgeon to dig it out? Somewhere in your mind, my young friend, is the memory of a technology that could allow me to reestablish contact once and for all!'

Sir Venus approached Acel with open clutching hands, salivating. Acel shrank back in fascinated horror.

'Where have our masters hidden the Gelatinous Cubes? There were eight of them ... Have they upgraded the system of TransmuCast? Oh, I've searched, searched this whole world over according to every pattern and code! I've tried, I've tinkered, I've attempted astral projection backwards—and how many wonderful things can I really do with the vestige of TransmuDream technology still left to me ... But my signals back merely distract, they do not inform! I have no communion with anything outside of what I can touch and feel! *I have no knowledge!* And you, what experience I wonder could an undeveloped dreamy youth like you have but a deliciously intelligence-permeated brainstem? You're like me, but you don't know as much as me ... and you never will. At least I have my pride. And I will never forgive those who would exile a sensitive genius and a true soldier like me and molly-coddle an abortion like you! Never! *Are you* a real man? I will never forgive them. I do have my pride, you know. One wonders if someone like you could possibly summon the strength to grip the reins of a horned sun plunging into ... listening to the begging for mercy of the Enemy's minions while a spear goes berserk in your hand—ah!' Sir Venus's eyes were glazed for a moment in an ashen color and he shook his head violently. 'Let us go back into the Dome and explore, eh? A new perspective for us!'

Immediately they were walking through the silver boulevards where shops were opening and the daily business getting underway. Acel didn't know how they'd made so much progress so quickly, how they'd suddenly gotten here. He had to trot after Sir Venus, who walked like a bull's charge. A guy with a huge moustache scowled at Acel when he stumbled around some crates being unloaded. An exotic female held his attention through the crowd a moment a star in his confusion. Everywhere noise and shouts of work and business as wide metal doors were flung up and wares being sold in explosions of drab colors and acrid smells. Acel was reeling.

'The Domed street of fat human intercourse,' Sir Venus explained ahead of him with an eternal oratory gesture.

'Really moving,' Acel muttered, but he thought, 'I can't admit any weakness to this bully, sure. Not remembering things that must've just happened. I feel like I'm drunk. How he hell did we get here?'

They maneuvered around open crates of pale cabbage substitutes. Accents and dialects of those who'd gathered in the Outskirts for the everlasting interests of survival and business ricocheted and streaked the air. An incredibly inspirational lovesong broke into their bodies from someone's TransmuCast. Sir Venus before him was once again old-looking and spoke cheerfully childlike, 'Let's proceed to a lower layer!'

'Whatever you say, Sir Venus.'

Acel wanted to buy time with blasé comments while he thought it out. He had to show that he was a capable physical person, not just a friendless waif lost in obscure eccentric books over his own disgust with the obesity and boring sexual terror of the Dome.

'What an awful man! He has a lot of Secret History perspective, I guess that's great … He certainly has his own style of talking, like an old book I'm not sure I want to read. But how could I ever take him seriously—the more I experience him, the more I fear he's losing the battle to a violent side I don't want to see.'

They had instantly turned into an extremely wide boulevard flanked by powerful pointed edifices of steely concrete—the Business Cones of the Dome's Incorporated Faction Government Area—Acel recognized it from a million images shown throughout his life, and he knew that it was impossibly far for them to have walked. Reality did not seem to be cooperating and Acel felt strange, somehow still gripping his intelligence by suspecting it was all a dream. He stared about himself like a man with more than tremendous interest in his surroundings, like an absurd archaeologist. Each one of the vast black buildings was adorned with immense corrugated ebony pillars and altar-like statues of faceless titanium beings of anonymous incontestable ideal strength. Some of the images held archaic tools of agriculture, others of geometry, some of war, but they did not resemble anyone who had ever lived near the Outskirts, as far as Acel could remember.

'Are these the gods and their houses?' he asked grasping at his old sardonic tone.

'No, they are squares. They are not Cubes.'

While Acel pondered over this bizarre answer Sir Venus led him up into the nearest one of these blank palaces, through an opaque plexiglas door.

'Welcome to the beerhall,' Venus snickered.

They entered a vast metallic hall into a cloud-rush of sound and sensation more dense than in a gigantic beehive, with shoeheels stamping, voices of all orders, perfumed odors, electronic squeals, stabbing penlights and jumbled up tunes. So many masses moving so rapidly, so ponderously, so loudly! In terrific quantities on many levels of railed floors far below and high above in blaring lights. Smooth-faced tight black suits stretched over various obesities strode to and past heavily and aggressively over the immense center floor and over all the cataracts. Similarly clad females wound over-voluptuously amidst them exhausting Acel with erotic untouchable super-elegance and velocity, and perfumes!—and he realized he did not exist to any of them. His breath came in gasps. Who do they love, his body desperately wailed, these progressive manikins who can't even read much less see themselves in the mirror while shaving? *I* am fit! Acel's jealousy became enormous as a famished cur sniffing the only bone in a kennel.

'That's the spirit, Sultan,' Sir Venus uttered low behind him, then changed his voice softly dramatically, 'Compassionate and merciful ...'

Acel grew sluggish, his body erupting various lewd mind-activity and passions and pities, they floated through the echoing chamber of collectively pained lusts—Acel could've sworn a whispered word swam over and over the din: mindsex, mindsex, mindsex is all you'll get, Poorboy.

'There is a grisly natural rightness here, Sir Venus, a selection—'

'Maybe so.' They stood near a facade of elevators vomiting and sucking human suits. There was no ceiling as far as Acel could see, it seemed to go up forever in crowded layers, catwalks, balconies, lit brighter than outside; below in wide terraced pits, the same. 'Do you know, a few of these fatboys here in this reversed chasm—those at the utmost level—have never been sick a day in their lives, they have never broken a bone, acquired a skin rash, nor suffered any emotional tragedy other than having their elaborate parents' bodies enshrined in cryogenic display cases …?'

'What? Are those true?'

Sir Venus ignored him. 'Oh, I expect to have an appointment with them all collectively one of these fine days. The Conscience of the Dome! Permanent fixtures. They are the only ones in the whole place who have what you could describe as enough. Yes, they still have enough. They're not running out of anything, like all the rest of you are! Do you envy that? They pull the strings of the wasting economy in this Dome, and become more hardhearted everyday! But I'll meet them once I am the master, and we'll have a bit to talk about while I appoint my viceroys. But for now their desultory attendance occurs on the highest levels of these towers with a view that gazes over the Dome's denizens in exultating grandeur at the power-pleasure which Fortune has been granting them for as long as history is able to tell them, and history can speak volumes for a good price. But perhaps I am speaking disrespectfully. I should say, gazing over the interesting proposition between themselves and God that has been personally negotiated with them each one—since that is the common tendency among those who rule.'

Acel's posture became very straight, tense.

'But do not develop a naïve attitude toward progress and capital, my young friend. Envy is a vice. Ambition needs perspective, that's all. Where is the eccentric who would rather see his mother and sisters raped and his father and brothers murdered, rather than shop for commodity essentials at a local convenience store? Imagine such a fanatic! I would like to caress his strange inhuman face with my fingernails. He has no love for himself, no concept of our extended natural community, no reality. Our empires are empires and must be measured by their relative brutalities and freedoms. Our talents must always be trained and used, and are. I myself have seen so many forms of human desire, Acel. I have analyzed the evidence of prehistoric civilizations more advanced than any you've ever seen, and the sunken continents and desert sheets of atomic blast-fused green glass they left behind ...'

Astonished, Acel was about to ask for once and all, Who *are* you, when suddenly the vast hall went black. A cacophony of squeals, nervous giggles, curses, blasé declarations and guffaws erupted around them in a desperate and apparently familiar void. Another momentary power failure had occurred, as it did time to time lately in the degenerating Domes. The great space felt as if filled with fleeing bodies yet sound betrayed that every single person was standing still, waiting with a secretly increasing anxiety.

The ragged seconds dragged on ponderously. The sound of a woman stifling tittering sobs burst near them. The black air was dense with various heavy breathings from heavy odiferous bodies. Acel imagined it was descending from every quadrant. He imagined he was naked. He imagined they all were, and they were rolling on top of each other in a huge screaming sighing heap. Somewhere there were angry grunts as someone thrust himself through others randomly—

'Society breaks down very quickly,' Venus muttered disgustedly.

Catching on his words like a life-raft, Acel asked, 'But what about the Homeguard?'

'They'll be at home protecting their wives!' Sir Venus gruffed and dragged Acel's arm somehow through the hideous crowded void into the blinding street. The day was still on. Traffic as almost normal. Amidst a few minor frustrations.

VIII

Contrary to TransmuCast report etiquette, which Captain Rice doesn't care about any more than Captain Rice is forced to now, it is in our best interests to analyze the history of agent known as Krystal Elioud as mentioned in Pleides Arrowhead Taurus (PAT), who was designated to enter Deeply Privileged with Captain Rice, we being the two closest relatives to human life of most appropriate service and rank. As you have probably noticed, we did not enter simultaneously, and not even in the same family. I am sending this in Special Velocity, normally reserved for Emergency as you know Major Bunder, so I cannot be sure where it will wind up in my full report, which I pray reaches you in good health. You have a reputation as a very patient man, which I hope may be true.

But first a word: it is not within scope of my report to repeat details of the moment I became aware of and able to TransmuCast these signals. That may be conjectured from their totality. I will continue to resist the temptation to utter personal comments on the hardships of Deeply Privileged which may be disparaging to general morale, doing as I have always done, although I realize that Special Velocity messages are translated through your office before any others.

Krystal Elioud Temporary Agent (re: PAT) is on record in earliest traceable existence a human female. This identification emerged before adequate historical research on the planet of human origins; that is, she was a prehistoric human creature relative to the mind that was later known, even by our Scribes, as human. Our physical anthropology department has strewn together—common knowledge—a pretty accurate picture of development here, although it must be admitted, vast millennia occur between every clue. We did not and do not have exact psychological references. And I have never heard from her on Earth, despite my searches and beacons. The purpose of this Special Velocity is to impart what I have only now thinly traced of her through arcane pages.

She was the last of the family Elioud, which was an ancient and unholy crossbreeding, six-fingered, gigantic and exceedingly beautiful descendents of the mighty Nephilim who migrated from a doomed continent during the wars which sought to exterminate them. Their impudence was legendary, their disregard for the lesser beings was intolerable, the offenses unforgivable. Finally a comprehensive genocide was agreed upon and launched by certain serious men, with the apparent blessings of angels and nature. Surrender to a horrible appetite which we love almost best; though our adversaries were not lacking in talent or means. This revolution spawned the bloodiest episode in ancient history and resulted in an erasure of almost all human knowledge acquired up to then. Aerial craft weapons technology of nuclear fire unleashed global catastrophes across the broken continents. Great cities were incinerated in a hail of exploding cosmic rays, populaces dropping with frozen smiles where they stood, furious glacial waters poured over the agriculture—civilization smothered. The remnants of our human race cowered in rags and caves but kept fighting, kept living; most did not understand what was happening to the world! Splashes of repercussive inferno had driven the giants into underground cities hiding for millennia, hardly to be ever seen again. The effects of this war were comparable to natural periodic purges, the carbon cycle annihilation or the meteoric destruction of dinosaurs, or even TransmuDream itself, for all parties involved.

The family's movements from those ancient days to the TransmuDream period are unknown. I strongly recommend reopening the files of the period. What you will find, I predict, is a history of no particular loyalty to the representatives of the human species they had long surpassed. And yet she had by the time become a Cosmic Ranger ... with a mysterious past. Major Bunder, perhaps this was not, or could not have been understood or taken into account during her assignment to Deeply Privileged. Perhaps it is not my business to ask. I myself did not conceive of it then, since before commitment … until today and my discovery of a strange album in this cold Outlanders' library. The names of others appear as well. Before now I had little idea of what such a mind's experience could mean translated immediately into the human world of the second Megalopolis.

IX

'That blackout sort of put me in the mood, how about you?' Sir Venus suddenly queried Acel. His voice was becoming more gravelly, his gestures more violent and bizarre. Some liquid ran down his pink chin, an alarming picture.

They had been eating sausages and drinking beer at high little tables outside for hours watching the obese people pass, the Government offices belching out the black traffic of the Dome, and observing the external life of inner Megalopolis during its last long hours of existence in a dying civilization.

'Come on now! Intimacy is the order of the day to the unconfused. Are you coming with me, or are you staying here with the drones?'

Although increasingly wary, something in this suggestion refreshed Acel and sent a wild hope along the outer cortex of his brain. However Acel lived by the clock, an employed individual paid for his regular time. Acel liked to be comfortable in this relationship with his employers at the library, so he did the best responsible job he could. At the back of his mind trailed the hours of life and sleep before he must work again tomorrow, weighing against how much more he could take of Sir Venus.

They walked for a long time then, til evening and the promise of peace set in the Dome, through a matrix of dull streets: metal doors rolling down, tired arms closing brilliant or blackened shops, traffic petering out on unknown various junctions. To Acel's mind they had circumscribed widely back towards the Gates, but from a strange different angle. In fact in some turns they appeared to have traversed at least thousands of kilometers, through bizarre streets scented with languages unknown to him—but always skirting the Outskirts. At corners Venus gripped his fists in front of himself, pulling through the air with a hideous grimace, just as if he were dragging back the reins of some fierce war wagon. Leaping ahead continents like vast drawn curtains at a corner, the transitions made no sense. Unrecognizable Zones, unkempt, faraway. Unrecognizable transitions into unkempt poorer Areas of the Dome. Cracked black concrete alleyways stench and make no sense. Trash and bits of greasy plastics scattered over the city. Yellow dogs sleeping in the roads. Acel wondered what they ate. Two of them, a pale and a dinge, play wrestling in the cracked grey gutter. One tears the ear of the other between short fangs. A screaming whelp. The others rouse up with terror and pointed interest staring, trembling with the ensuing mortal fight. Several copulate in excitement.

Venus snorted at them and laughed, 'Who does this scene please?'

Most of the dogs now began tearing at the loser's hanging red flesh while he squirmed shrieking and crying pitifully like a child begging for mercy in a foreign tongue. But that only increased the savagery and bloodthirstiness.

'Listen to that,' Venus paused. 'The pure lovely innocence of childlike play, through an accident transformed into a cannibalistic holocaust.. We could stop it— but we don't. We wait and watch, just like they did at first. Just like our Masters do now, and they are so righteous! Should we follow their appallingly dispassionate example? After all, aren't they the ones who set the scene for our little picture show—maybe it's their right to get amusement from it. Tell me, is it so commendable to stand around like a wallflower watching the tortures of another when you have the cure within your grasp? If not in your grasp, certainly yours with a little effort! I wonder if you're even brave enough to consider these tortures with an un-TransmuCasted mind ... Has that suffering beast died yet—he must've known his time was up.'

Acel could not answer this. Then they had begun to move again, pulled ahead continents like vast drawn curtains at a corner, the transitions made no sense to him. Poorer sections of concrete blocks, giddy lighting and sentimental party song blasted from caves wreathed in sensuous glows. As they passed, darkness within and the inviting smiles of exotic homey enchantresses.

'This one's great,' Sir Venus explained and led them down into some dark joint. 'Thursday night's always wild, you get your carelessness ...'

A twinge about his next day's work filled Acel for a half-second—'Do I have time for this?'—the next he was drinking glasses of iced beer with two lovelies encouraging and assisting his comfort every moment of the way.

The club was dark and primitive. Low black tables were fixed between rows of hard red sofas. Amidst the loud barrage of TransmuCast karaoke amateurs drinking and copious flirting with the hired girls. Sir Venus sat across from him, not so very older, indulging himself in 5 different ways. Periodically he shouted something to him, boring messages he did not understand.

'My signal's merely obstruct, distract! I haven't got it right! I want to *inform*. Do you see? Your old friend hasn't been able to tell me either. What is the location, what is the code, how do I build such a device again rightly ...? You may even have a codename ... Somewhere in your brainstem. Do I have to tear it apart, eat it—I will, so help me! I don't know how you could be so cowardly dense. Cube, code, Cube, code! I could really help you out. Can't you think of it?'

'I'm a librarian, Sir Venus. I know book codes, a filing system, I don't know if that could help you ... *What* old friend?'

'No, you do not understand my frustration. You are still eons away from it. But just you wait. I have my pride, you know, and I will never forgive their misunderstanding. Never! The repetitions, the repetitions, the boredom of being locked in this stagnating world away from the scent of true conquest. E Gads!

Your namby-pamby fantasy world—*Megalopolis!'* he spat the word out and the women sprawled over his massive arms twitched in disgust with him. Still, they had to work; he wasn't deformed at least. 'I am fully aware that though I harry you, neither of you allow me. So I obstruct instead of communicating. And all I've got left is my pride! What else does a soldier have? But no, no, you don't allow me so I must obstruct. Neither of you. But maybe you will, you know? It took me longer to find you than the other. Oh, she barely fit in, wasn't molded to all this so well. I don't know how you didn't notice it when you used to learn in school together. A few others did, Good Lord!—the Enemy's minions had been on her trail every step of the way since her entry—you're lucky I got to her first, since you couldn't do a darn thing for her yourself, and still can't. *What* is your bunch thinking? Some things certainly haven't improved! The body of a woman at age 10—this is not usual for human females. Hey, I can read. I hear the majority of your intentions. My own invention isn't completely useless. All this information is rightfully mine anyway—I'm a veteran, too, like you probably were in your last life ... I had a good idea you would enter and in what form. But I cannot relate my experience of you, can I? I can't inform, can I? No, I can only sit here, in all the nobility of the best example of the species of this glorious planet and talk to *you!* And *you* don't even comprehend one darn little word I'm talking about! Like these primitive girls, you're all body with only the rudiments of a mind. You're not stronger than me in mind or body! Nobody born in this whole Dome is! So why shouldn't I have the same certain privilege as your dripping excuse for an investigation? I'm just considering what I want to do with you. How long has it been since I was abandoned by your betters and masters with a disenchanted force that would soon hate all restraint and authority? I have to discipline them even yet—when I find them. I have my pride, you know. But no, it's not accepted, I must be referred to as a Renegade! Me! Ignorance! How could I forgive it? How long has it been since the reins were yanked from *my* hands?'

Acel had been laughing insincerely for a long time. And yet he minded less and less. Anyway Venus seemed to be picking up the bill. It was a once in a lifetime experience! Yes, yeah, that's right, longtime! he shouted back while paying attention to many other more pleasant things and drinking glass after glass—

It was suddenly 10pm, and Acel began to consider intensely his increasing fun and the state of health absolutely required for tomorrow's work at 8am. He must rise at 7, so Acel figured compassionately that he had 2 more hours of good times before he had to go home to sleep. His body now enjoying so many caresses. His latest empty glass he placed gingerly on the table where it was filled again immediately by the obliging foxes … he let them go on … 'What am I thinking?' he said to himself flabbergasted as he chugged the nectar, 'It's only 10pm and I don't work til 8—Why, I've got 12 hours, not 2, loads of time!'

Let the karaoke amateurs sing on! More singing! More action! Acel wanted this night to last forever. He extricated out of the booth to go pee. The facilities were in a grimy backroom. Its door was a plastic frame covered with dirty plastic siding that closed clumsily. Time should stop, stop! What could be better than this whirl like a TransmuDream? He came back through the happinesses and loudness in the darkness. The current singer is fantastic, so sweet! But he remembered he did not really like to listen to music much anymore, what a mistake. Music's vibrations affect emotion so strongly; it can be taken in appropriate doses. Acel felt like a scientist—it was wonderful, perfectly appropriate! Before he sat down Acel also conceived that a kind of music could be designed of a combination of vibrations that would inspire the development of a soul—inspirational music. Did he get this idea from an old book? But now it was his own anyhow, Acel fell back satisfied, especially when it was only himself in the whole Dome who was hearing such mind-bombarding sounds. It was different thinking with all these girls here. They made him drunker and happier than he'd ever been in his life.

'You may be a sycophant, but I enjoy your society!' Venus shouted to Acel across the alcoholic valley between their exploits. Arm outstretched in heroic gesture, face vivid with triumphal delight, suits of brown layers, a vest the soft flame red of a mountain lion's nose. Brother, brother, older brother ... What is this strange pact you seem to want to be making with me, Mr Venus, my older brother? This woman, she has always been my sister-lover. And I must discuss things in getting to know her better.

Real flesh flashes. 'I'll never TransmuCast it again!' The rest of that night Acel Daniel could only contrive from a few glorious and embarrassing pictures left to his memory—it was wiped out amidst chaotic spaces. He had never been with a woman before. Dear wild multifarious embracings of a sweet special beauty in a room made just for them. Somewhere, in some prelude to acts of love, Acel's mind dawned with a new self-consciousness toward his purpose in his life, in all life. And as he fell one knee on the bed in an ecstasy of consummate naked abandon, he realized that Sir Venus was somewhere near in a similar pretty little room doing the same, but was not of the Domes.

X

Scenes of Megalopolis from far up and away—he was flying, skimming the concavity of the Dome—the deep combinations swam in Acel's dream before he was drawn down to where he last walked. He was stumbling outside looking for water, water found in a tremendous vat under a soft sky between lime green concrete alleys. It seemed to him that Sir Venus was behind him, commanding him, 'Make sure you know which vice is yours. One vice can stimulate life—more than that can destroy it. Do not allow your intelligence to be crushed by freedom.'

The rim of the vat spread out, and Acel was walking along a night beach with Sir Venus. They were dressed in archaic clothing. And yet the vat was in the sea, or was most of it; a huge brown creature lolled there with the shape of a man or a baby, or there were millions of people swimming making up its shape. There was a pounding, a beating, pounding coming from a billion hearts in the dark furious water—

Acel opened his eyes. The pounding came all around him. No, it was the door. It was flung open and Acel was on his feet struggling to pull on his clothes while Sir Venus was pulling him outdoors. If it was possible his red white and blue eyeballs flashed a glint even more maniacal than last night. Acel was barely able to shove a generously adequate number of money under some glass object on a bright yellow bedside table before he was dragged from the room, face fastened with a mixture of confusion at the still brown sleeping form he left behind.

'Yes, that's right, appropriate enough already, come on put your arm in that sleeve not your leg!' Sir Venus was shouting whispers at his ear with hog breath. 'This is no time to be experiencing nostalgic sentiments. We are being pursued, which due to the appalling nature of our pursuers makes it, makes it tenfold worse, my new dear little friend, and we must get the heck out of here now!'

'Thank you very much!' Acel shouted over his shoulder as they leapt stumbling down unknown slapdash stairs with a last pantleg flailing behind his ass. 'I'm being shanghaied by a fallen angel!'

'You are a gentleman and a fool,' Sir Venus told him and dragged him out into painful silver morning, increasing a sharp serious grip on his arm.

They left any semblance of a street. They were ascending in flying moonsteps up through a huge diaphanous ribbed tube. Grey, pink, its walls sheen with bright shadows. With Acel screaming as they lurched upward, they seemed to be searching for some place to rest or to be safe. The terrifying tube curved several times a vast distance out into space.

They lay in utter darkness.

Acel heard Sir Venus whisper beside him, felt the warm sour breath attack his own nostrils.

'We should not be here. I could not think of a better place to escape immediate danger. But we can not stay long and if we … if I am found here a worse suffering would follow … for me. Someone else might not think it so bad.'

The smooth glassine surface beneath Acel's body was cold, cold and black. He was surrounded in blackness that pressed his limbs down against the infinitesimally convex plain.

'Where are we? What's wrong with you?' Acel demanded.

'I must ask you to be silent! Have I ever continued talking when you have asked me to be quiet? *N-y-oooh.*' Venus once more sunk to that rotten childish mockery, his red face already quivering as the words slid out like worms with a disgusting taste. 'Have I ever pried into *your* personal life with incomparably probing rude questions? *Nyooh.*' It was so irrational. 'I *assume* you'll want to find out the answers to all your life's little questions sooner than I would prefer you to, *Mr Ranger*. Then my search for you, my waiting, all my watching will have been in vain, without a doubt, now wouldn't it? If there hadn't been a massive emergency I should keep you from the old secret places in the hollow mist between worlds just like this here. Ah, the views those Watchers must have had from up here, amusing oneself with our species' poor masochism. You'd never have seen these old stomping grounds until I am ready to return in undreamed of power—of course with only one of us in command. One has to accept traditional spiritual feudalism, which I am more capable of than you. What's a soldier without his pride? That is, if I haven't polluted my spiritual stock with my over-attention to you. You are a high maintenance acquaintance. But I doubt if that thought ever entered your namby-pamby fantasy world. No, now you are still innocent, an unblemished white rose, and you can grow in any garden you find yourself in. You *will* be trained. Your reports will be shaped as they should.'

The blackness had not cleared; it weighed on every presence of Acel's mind. All he could feel was Venus's warmth stretched beside him, repulsively.

'Look, I don't know what the hell you're talking about, and I am obviously dreaming. So I would like to get whatever I want! Give me more women! Fried food! Wine! Magical powers!'

'Idiot! All you've ever wanted is all the books you can eat. I insist you please shut up! I'm sorry to be rude, but you really have to shut up. Magical powers are already somewhere in your brain, by your infantile standards. If I could take that from you ...'

Venus's voice was low and wild, Acel shrank away from him in the void. He did not have to see that face to know how terrifying it was, but he didn't have the strength to rise from this cold plain.

'Consider yourself lucky that we haven't time for a proper operation. We must prepare to return to the Earth. We are being hotly pursued by two ... They are ... They are soul enslavers who will give you no choice, destroy you with a few opposing obsessed passions pingponging back and forth—that's their meat. You won't get any perspective from them, that's for sure. I have attempted to record their names several times before but the memory is consistently stolen from me by my own fate, which I hope someday you may understand. One of them is able to transform its shape into any shadow it wishes. The other carries an evil book in which he scribbles any word dear to the human race and smothers it with curses. They are Renegades now, if that's the right word for it, though they never stray from each other and hate all other contact. Pillow-biters, if you ask me. Under what circumstances would a man be biting a pillow? Think about it. Those twins out of Egypt. You would recall their names with sentiment and distaste, if your memory was what it should be.' His voice became grim. 'You must teach me the Cube with which you used to report them. Or is there a new code, a new codename?'

As Venus spoke, far away in this strange lack of light Acel became aware of a tiny glistening flower of soft color emerging, slowly growing closer, exuding such a loving warmth and enormous attraction, and Acel longed to be off, away with it somehow, away from this violent sinister voice.

'They each have an ancient history. You'll have to try to think. They're descended from the royal line of a parallel and more essential realm that once had seen better days. Their own mother once reclined in this very place, watching ... before she reclined with many others below, further below, and above. Those old books you like to pursue might've mentioned them. Now their present lot is a far cry from what they once were. But they're still dangerous to me ... and you.'

There was a repulsive hiss—Sir Venus had noticed the change in Acel's attention. Suddenly they were falling through, Acel was plummeting, or reality was rushing up past him, he was not moving except for the flinging up of limbs in terror. Like a watercolor the matter of a lightly wooded hill spread up around him covered in freezing snow. Snow! He staggered in its soft sloping ground, in cold winter weather under a faint pink sunless sky. Acel had never seen real snow before, and he had surely never felt anything so cold! Granite rocks and black trees twisted up the slope in clannish patches. Sir Venus was before him further down, still in his strange soupy brown layers of suits. His red hair stood on end like a male baboon. The next things Acel witnessed improbably with a vision that amazed him—

Two dark figures swept up at Sir Venus and they were immediately engaged in fierce combat. The three-way sound of the impact echoed down and far around the little valleys. Acel could not imagine why this was going on. A vicious fight ensued, not untouched by a martial form of elegance which Acel found bewilderingly attractive. The blackened skin of the one interposing with the repulsively brilliant hue of the other, both tearing at Sir Venus's parrying form—his limbs moved like lightning.

An intense dread overwhelmed Acel til he cowered down panting like a rabbit, burying himself in the deep stinging snow. In a streak of vision he perceived the two demons forced back by Sir Venus's fists. Slurred words issued from the huge man's mouth in a blur. Sweat ran copiously from him and Acel almost pitied him then, horrified by his attackers. In terror he clawed toward the white earth. A malicious shadow leapt to and fro lunging at Venus and was barely beaten back before a creature with skin more livid than a nauseating sunset calmly dealt him wicked furtive blows and retreated with hideous arrogance.

Their visages were inconceivable and assaulted Acel's mind in cruel nightmare as he strove to watch this fight. He had no doubt that a horrible doom would tear him to bits were the hero he had found so repulsive to fail now. How he thanked and prayed for and almost worshipped Venus's strength and wild aggression at this moment—anything to save him from these monsters.

In one second Acel was filled with relief when they leapt away into the sky, and with dismay as Venus leapt after them. They landed together in the duned desert farther away than an eagle's keen sight. Acel did not understand how he could see these things, he did not want to. He must have been dreaming a nightmare awake—a sensation that must've somehow come from Venus—or did it? His mind felt drunk, totally free. It was in ecstasy. But it was an ecstasy of horror. With a sudden longing he wished to be away living in a green field he had never seen, playing with crowlike birds who came curiously to nose him—and he did not know where this thought came from either. He saw Sir Venus land with a quake in the spilling dune five thousand kilometers away. The Red Twin awaiting him there opened his hand and a line of corrosive fire stretched forth exploding toward him in the sand. Venus was hurled back in torment. Though Acel didn't realize that he'd filled his lungs with desert air as he fell back, Venus suddenly exhaled a powerful long gust blowing a sheet of sand into the evil eyes of his two enemies.

Sir Venus leapt away this time, farther than an elephant's low frequency reception—though Acel was doomed to hear and see every step, by what power he could not conceive! Venus landed amidst treetops, in a land unlike Acel had ever seen. He had never seen the sea outside of dreams and TransmuCast, but here it was sprawled blue like a billion-handed open-palmed breathing creature larger than the world's belly. The sound of it was rushing all around his ears. Sir Venus sprung across the flexible pinetops, bouncing one to the other in long strides til he landed in the low surf. The tall thin trees behind him a faint pinkish hue, their biology long shattered in a TransmuDream aftermath. They seemed warmer at a human touch and breath.

But soon enough Venus's pursuers landed, and the waters steamed away or grew fetid where they stepped. The Shadowy One dove headlong into the sea where he was invisible circling behind. Only some turning up of dead fishes and fleeing crablife betrayed his course. Meantime the Red Twin approached slowly and boldly from the mutant forest chuckling sinisterly.

'It is a pleasure to see you again, Sergeant,' he intoned in a rasping oven-hot breath.

'The pleasure's all yours, your Grace. I preferred the hospitality of your dissipate palace below, bizarre as it was.'

'Alas, Hermosa saw her doom with the cowardly abduction of our Viceroyess—may her cherished memory long be preserved—stolen away by a nascent Cosmic Ranger,' the Red Creature winced in shades of flame, and from the hillside many kilometers away Acel believed that there was in fact something noble about this monster, or once was. What did Venus say, Egyptian dukes who are not what they once were ...? Yes, there *was* an ancient dignity and power in the Red Duke's aspect that Acel could not help feeling himself attracted to. Indeed he was almost abashed at the uncouth manner in which Venus laughed in his face.

'Abducted, did you say? Ah, your Grace, that is rich! As rich as the putrid smells of the corridors of Hermosa's hall covered in the feces of many various species for your entertainment. What an amazing family! Your many-breasted mother was abducted alright, abducted by her well-known lust for new meat I'd say—that's how the Beatrix fled from a neglected and dying realm with that neophyte. Now nobody knows where she is, including you. That's what happened. The true history of events! What real man doesn't know the unalterable nature of you lower gods, disgusting offspring of demons and fallen angels? Just like the heart of a tiger, your appetites are insatiable, crawling.... It was just the same way, if you care to remember, with your fabulous sister too, the so-called Rose of Beatrix, who 'fled' and was 'abducted' at about the same time—'

The Red Duke tightened like a cord of white heat, 'How dare you let those names pass your inferior lips—'

'Ah yes. Who would've expected I'd do something like that? Well, pardon me, she *was* a gem, just like her mother. And who could expect that the fecund Rose of Beatrix, this luscious sister of yours, would've been hypnotized into grotesque acts of love with the Golem you'd once created to recapture her, to subdue her, to destroy her ecstatic abandon and send her back to fat Mama's cage below the universe, back to your bizarre sexual predation. I guess you didn't expect that either! Imagine. Unchained and free, the most attractive and alluring creature in the Cosmos copulating on Earth with the most repugnant artificial being. A green homunculus! Did it make you jealous?' Venus shouted at the darkred princely figure, to Acel's horror. 'Did it? Did you? Incestuous disgusting lower gods. Lusting after the loveliest of my species too. Always when we were in a weakened state, in our primeval beginnings, or after TransmuDream ... '

Sir Venus lifted his fingers in defamatory gestures.

'Viceroyess, huh? Beatrix, huh? Your spoiled mother has other names, like soul sucking Succubus, Adam's Ex, the Original Bitch, Lilith the Baby Snatcher, ManEater, Lola Dominatrix—Lola always gets what she wants. Our mistress of despairing obsession! That's her history of criminal lust. Exiled in the holes of a desert dust. Thousands of bastards spawned a day from every leering toad, foaming snake, mincing wasp and passing ghost. No one could ever forget her. Vaginal secretions like a neon gum sticking passions to objects—and no one could ever forget them!. Our mistress of idolatries. How many petty obsessions has she spawned with her universal secretions, tearing human lives apart in hotpink yearnings? How many melancholies, livid regrets, specters, bizarre dreams, neuroses, depressions, self-hatreds, paranoias, suicidal implosions and ridiculous alienating losses of temper and self-respect? How many times have we succumbed, not recognizing reality for the gummy sauce she tried to cook us in? Wasting our time with self-deception. The criminal history of your insidious family.'

Thunder rolled over the sea and a light phosphorous rain fell on them there.

'Are you quite finished with your own tedious disrespect, Sergeant?'

'Yes, yes, please,' Acel whispered gripping the snow far away.

'Not one for the good old days, eh your Grace? You and your insane twin were born about that time too, weren't you, when your mother laid freely on the Red Sea shore, come what may? Do you know which one your own father was? I sure do! The unrepentant idealist who taught grand secrets to my species—well, to the women of my species that his associates took for their own … Don't think I'm not appreciative, your Grace. I see two sides of the coin when you're always trying to shove me only one. That hideous crossbreeding produced an impressive race who were scientists in their way, and their advanced sciences of war and love were disseminated all over this dull little ball of dirt. Really livened up the place. Certain circles just didn't see the beauty of sharing Art with the common apes of Earth, that's all. And you tell me not to name names! Your absurd names! In payment for it, a real Noble One who's name I actually *do* fear to mention strapped him upside down in chains like a screaming goat outside the window of your Egyptian baby cradle … And this is the history of a Watcher! A sleepless Grigori! Azazel! Azazel! how beautiful was your face before the fingers of lust manipulated the muscles of your bronze lips! Before you gave up serene service for the alluring females of a lower more hungry order … This is the behavior we get from your family! Terrible history. Viceroyess! Your Hermosa was a mockery. A syndrome during our weakness. I could not say so as your slave then …'

'I warned you to hold your tongue—' the Red Duke glowed with menace of immeasurable depth. 'You are not so clean, little man, not so pure, not so free. You know that I taste daily the in's and out's of your own—what was your term?— sexual predation.'

'Oh, forgive me, your Grace. You would instruct me in conscience, of course, another of your fine arts. I would like to listen, but it's difficult to escape the absolute fact that your kind is a mere syndrome! Arrogant! A syndrome, a mockery of a government, a parody of a mind where opposites oppose to the most ridiculous extremes. Hurling us between hate and love like insects. Blinding us to our freedom. Obsessing us. Enslaving our souls. Are you in league with the Enemy? Humans have always been the herd you fed from! You feed from the destruction caused between the conflict of opposites. You ignore the creative side. And you can't even control your own appetites, none of you! But who would've expected the incorrigibly fecund nature of your sister would've even swung so low as to breed with that pet Golem of yours, producing the most myriad reptilian hordes which burned so many farms, laid waste to settlements, nearly pushed people back into caves playing with little broken chiseled rocks! Just when we had *nothing* after our TransmuDream crisis! We were trying to rebuild ourselves!'

'Then it serves you right, doesn't it?'

The Red Duke had perhaps cooled his temper, he even sniffed contemptuously down his long sanguine nose. But Acel far away noticed the subtler glance over Sir Venus's right shoulder toward his approaching black brother. His mouth moved in impotent horrors of warning.

Meanwhile Venus had become even more livid with rage and finally that sickeningly insane sarcasm.

'Serves us right, you say! We deserve it? Give me more agony, I'm still so alive! Itch, itch, itch, your kind never stop! I command this, you say! I command that, you say! Pushing us around like rats in a maze! ... Have I ever judged *your* conscience with impossible ideals? Have I ever reduced everything you cherish to a failed mathematical equation, and then ripped the reins from your hands just as you were mounting the highest star? Have I ever blinded one eye and then the other on off on off alternately while you battled at full spirit's gallop with the temptation of the Enemy, which even *you* must contend with, sickening Duke. And *have I ever* betrayed you with false support and ignored you while I was lost in my own self-indulgent pleasureous fantasy while you were struggling with the lowest orders of life?! ... *Nyooooh.* So why do you do it to me?'

Venus just had time to jab his thumb into his burly chest before he was leapt upon from behind by a shape of wet shadow. Manta-like wings enclosed his screaming struggling body in obscene angles. The Red Duke sniffed again with a derisive grimace. The grey tide washed back out but Venus held his ground, bracing his feet in the damp sand. With a herculean effort he launched himself straight into the sunless sky. The shadowy twin clinging behind. Acel had almost lost sight of the clutched figures up in the dull pink cumulous when he saw the sanguine twin follow, firing up like a mortar. Up, fighting as they went, Sir Venus dragged the awful dukes of Egyptian ghost desire and lust, respectively ... For long minutes they flew away up, and disappeared in some window in the sky.

XI

Her window wasn't large. It wasn't barred. It was a deep sharp rectangle in the stone which brought to Diona the mirror faces of the prisoner's grief and the redundant voice of the perpetual captive.

Across from her, further than she could throw anything in her cell, but close enough to see every feature and grimace of Rachel Cruz's beautiful face, her childhood friend's tower stood. Rachel was peering through her own window now, her lovely dark eyes gazing back at her. A seamless slit in a bare needle. A belt of towers jutting round the broad descending broken steps of a vast lava flow hundreds of kilometers wide. It's frozen surface gleamed in filthy ebon of brittle ash. Rachel's window was the only one she could see clearly, though there was at least one other tower visible but too far to make out its sad inhabitant. And Rachel could make out someone else's behind hers, she knew, because they had between them created a living cuneiform of hugely angled facial and body gestures in order to communicate what their voices couldn't sustain nor their eyes articulate. But Diona's eyes couldn't reach anyone but Rachel effectively. They had nothing to say to each other now, they were just watching each other's faces, staring into another life.

Certainly over ten years they'd had but few messages to send, messages of loneliness and love. And continued confusion usually—over the strange books and food that were brought to them, over the reason for their captivity, over their helplessly changing bodies, and especially over their captor, whose visits with them were always never less than a cruel swing between bizarre delight and savage bitterness, despair.

One day Rachel had made strange gestures to her. At first Diona believed that she was referring to the intimate activities each of them had with their captor since they were first brought here, that strange magical day—their captor he remained in their minds, though their affections were so oft sweetly aroused in pleasure and desperate loneliness; neither were so stupid as never to dream of the freedom they once had and could not have now. How near was this captivity to that species of honey'd tyranny which leaves only oneself to blame? The tower and the locked door were real. But the door opened from time to time—and their dream of freedom was sweetly poisoned. Yet captor he remained. No woman, however shallow or sheltered, is such a fool as not to intimate the unchecked urge of a man. His is an ever-expanding power. Only the adept female can survive, or even flourish, and still love. And in truth he had never given them his name; he had only laughed, loud and long, when asked so many million times. He'd said that they couldn't pronounce it, or they'd never love him once they'd heard how absurd it was. He'd steered them this way for years. And sometimes in a jocular mood he suggested they just call him My Lord. He had made love to them since they arrived.

And then Diona thought her beautiful friend must be referring to the personal thing that had not happened to them simultaneously, but now did, the pain and the blood that flowed from their insides at almost equal periods. They were grown up women now, they knew—though Diona had known this discomfort secretly for far longer, it was hard to remember a time before it began. But they did not understand the internal causes of this regular woe. The moon above seemed to count their days as he turned his face dreamily. Their only confidant. They tore bits of pages counting the days, while he did up above so slowly, and they used every replenished supply of soft cloth to keep their bodies clean.

In fact they were well provided for. Diona's cell was full of cushioned and pretty furniture such as she had never known before. Warm water flowed from pressurized taps. An ice-fan blew adjustably. Delicate clothings, soaps, enchanting cosmetics, stuffed animals, paints, pretty little amusing books and toys, and especially various foods were slipped through a trap in the door whenever they slept—nothing was not delicious and always seemed quite what Diona would've chosen herself. But they had not once been able to fool or discover whoever did it. It must've been the Lord. Only he could've been so subtle.

Diona stood naked in the window's heat. She was pale and beautiful, slim and voluptuous. She thought back to the last time her Lord had visited her. The door opened, as it always did, by wonderful magic. Barely perceived, the curling stair behind which Diona never had a chance to descend. In a half moment he was embracing her. The rough brown folds of his cloak surrounded her warmly. At once she was loved again. The whispers of My Lord with the caustic chemical breath of the wines he drank, which she could never quite get used to, always the same, and she always softened.

'Out, out—don't you ever think of getting out of here, my little sister?'

These were different words than usual, but Diona gave no sign of noticing it. She leaned back in his embrace. 'Where could we go? Look outside—nothing but wasted metallic plains where nothing grows.'

The Lord thrust her from him. 'Have I *ever* deprecated your intentions? Have I *one time* eaten away at the security of your paradise by pointing out obvious trifles on purpose to make you feel stupid? Have I ever reminded you of your immature intelligence when it was so easy to convince you to come here in the first place?' His face was already palpitant with a feeling so extreme he could only articulate it with the illogics of an inner obsession. His tongue raked so slowly and heavily along the upper cavity of his mouth, with a sickenly childish mocking expression, '*Nyooh*. Then why do you do it to me now?'

This was a disgusting mood Diona had rarely glimpsed in her captor. Her face softened toward him.

'I have always totally believed in your beatific intention. I have always thought of you as My Lord because you are a good man. You take care of me while the world dies.'

'It will not die, my little sister!' He took her hands in his before his searing lips. 'You are forgivably ignorant of the fact that in each of these 444 blessed towers I have raised an angel, less beautiful than you but with purpose, and in each of them except one I have finished planting my seed. A nice job, if I say so myself. It has taken some time and there are many already who enjoy the dearest company of the fulfilled maternal goal—and myself as a sturdy provider. Ah, but you should imagine the contentment I now feel surveying a solid plain clustered with the separate pinpoints of my heart's desire, in such an abundant number! Each tower a planet of various joy and pleasure. So many long years have I dwelt in patient increase of power. And to know that I am capable of keeping you all safe and prosperous here until the Domes fade in their dying power supply that I've mentioned so often. Then, yes, then the world is ours my dear—and we will steer it in a direction which truly rivals the gods!'

Diona did not remember her captor ever revealing so much of his mind to her. Some of his speech was difficult to follow and she echoed, 'Maternal goal?' before he again seized her shoulders hotly and spoke with that new frightening patronizing intensity.

'You *know* there is only one thing missing, just as there is only one female yet unimpregnated. I have waited so long indeed. I am going to ask you once more very clearly if there isn't somewhere in your deepest memory some conception of a transmitting machine, a technology allowing us to broadcast our very thoughts to the Multiverse at large? Like a dream that reaches everyone in the same night. You must see what that could do for our new empire. Have you never had such an idea?'

Diona looked into her captor's sharp blue eyes. It was true that he had asked similar questions ever since she had been brought here—she and Rachel had signaled about them with a finger drilling into an open hand. But again she could imagine nothing that he was talking about that really dwelt in her mind. Only the closed door behind them forever remained in her thought. Diona's exquisite face did not waver in her tranquil dependant expression.

'Sometimes I wonder at the shallow duplicitousness of females. I guess you have no choice.' the Lord muttered. 'Well, I've saved you for last. Though you were ready first. And I'll save you a bit more too. I guess I'll ask these same stupid questions again too. Something about you, sweetheart. You're my last hope, save one. I wonder if I should bring you together ...' he finished and looked toward the door. Diona stood and watched him flee through it with words of promises she had learned to forget.

And now it dawned on Diona's mind what it was that Rachel was signaling to her: she was pregnant like the others, and it was a fearful thing. Neither of them really understood what it would all entail, except that Rachel would suffer separate from her—very much. Rachel had been sick recently pretty often. This was it. Diona did not know whether to hope or to dread what this all now meant.

XII

A pressurized silence, Acel's ears were stinging with the cold. Acel strained his attention to an invisible point in the discolored cumulous covering the sky. He was drenched in pouring sweat, burning snow stuck all over him like freezing paint. Acel wanted to flee away so badly he would've left his brains behind—but where? He glanced around wildly on the slope, it was just like more of the same: snow covered white hills, scrubby dying oakish trees scant and bent. As far as he could see. He didn't even know if he was on the same continent as home. Acel thought of his mother there, sitting, absorbing the TransmuCast, worrying about him as she did every single day—and he pushed himself up and on.

Acel crossed the hillsides jaggedly, trying to stay close to the pitiful trees. He was so thirsty, so famished, he tried squeezing the moisture out of handfuls of snow which bit his hands. He even tried breaking off the most lifelike twigs to chew or sucking at the torn dry little branch remaining, and he imagined he got just a little something, but not enough.

Mostly Acel simply tried not to think. He was too close to delirium. He threaded and staggered his way carefully as he could, wanting to get far away and out of this terrible snow. But even so, his mind exploded with memory tangled in fantastic conjecture, attempting beyond his will to make sense of what had happened since yesterday.

The recurring conclusion that Venus intended some horrible malice beneath his invitations was unavoidable. The man was so unpleasant, it was hard to think of him as anything but a maddened bandit of some kind, regardless of how much piteousness so often emerged between his ugly temper and childish mockeries. 'That guy's nuts!' He was large enough to be pretty frightening too, most of the time. And Acel didn't care for being constantly relegated to a life of artistic idiocy in rude language either, even if his fears were unfounded. Acel's sensitivity and intelligence had usually in his life commanded a particular respect from the others he'd had to deal with over time—among his old school peers, his few work colleagues and even his tennis friend Nik—just as you *would* speak to someone whom you realized was more intelligent (which disguises itself as vast experience) than you, and who was yet miraculously sympathetic to your frustrations as being much the same as his own. And Acel's sardonic humor had more than once carried the day, or the night. Since practically everyone was always caught up evening after evening in the rapid exciting TransmuDream projections, anyone with any skill with words could awe his fellows with a bare twist on perspective or even by just deftly aiming a couple long and efficient words at a given situation. They were easily awed and won over, although because of Acel's inward nature he had never to his knowledge ridden any crests of popularity, and he hadn't. All the same, he wasn't really used to huge violent men threatening him with cosmic subjects and brain dissection! He wasn't used to apparent teleportation or brothels (though on reflection that didn't seem so bad). He wasn't used to mortal combats with hideous monsters seen in clairvoyant vision either. And as for trudging lost in a snowy wilderness in a strange land, he could not admit that he liked it at all. Pursuing an intellectual secret 8am to 5pm in a musty abandoned library seemed much more pleasing right now than this.

Acel's head swam on. He believed at least he was not suffering anymore displaced visions. His legs began to lose their feeling, like jelly; at times he became terrified he was also losing his knowledge of how to walk, how to move one leg after another in a coordinated locomotion, and was forced to drag his body and hurl himself from one scraggly trunk to another drunkenly, filled with waning desperation. The next tree loomed ahead of him dancing with its clan. This had always been their happy joy. They joined long knotty fingers on lithe limbs cavorting in circles as the hillside grew dark.

A little white fox in the brambles watched Acel stagger and roll down the next hillside. 'Not very clever!' he thought, twitching his nose. 'Doesn't know his way around.' Another conceited sniff and he bounded off thinking he had a good idea of where to find a nice bunch of little eggs he could get for almost free.

XIII

Acel awoke weakly but refreshed. The air was crisp but he was not freezing. He was wrapped in stiff heavy plastic on a hard floor. And then he noticed the bars. The dull pink sky behind seemed more distant than ever. He was lying in a wooden cage.

Acel sat up with a start. Behind him squatted another man, whom apparently shared his cage. About the same age and size as Acel, maybe younger, thicker, with brown hair and a square clean face and moustache, gazing upon Acel with softly chiseled eyes that emanated such sincerity and feeling that at first and often later Acel found himself looking away. But his strange cellmate said nothing, only gazing, gazing with a sympathy Acel found almost too intense.

'Where are we?' Acel ventured.

'I'm sorry?' the stranger asked with an accent Acel had never heard.

Acel gazed around outside the cage at huts and houses built of black twisted wood, obviously from the scant trees on the hills he'd come from, and white thick plastic sheets. He spoke again slower, louder.

'Where are we? You, me—Where?'

'Far away from the Dome.' The stranger answered. His voice was melodious, warm even, with an arrestingly deep voice. He spoke correctly, but again with an unfamiliar accent.

At this point Acel's exhaustion and starvation began to overpower him again. He felt his face crumble into tears and he could not speak.

'That a boy, now, that a boy. I can tell you haven't seen much of the hard life, but maybe too much too soon. Well, maybe you're warm, aren't you? You'll get some food in a while. That's as far as I go myself. But maybe you'll enjoy the other duties of nature soon to be pressed upon you. Disgusting to me, probably not to you.'

Acel swung his head around and looked again through the black bars at the snowy hills. He noticed after a short while that he'd been filled with calm and a placid disinterest in the tears he'd just shed. He watched a short slender woman come from one of the white huts holding something in her hands. She was all wrapped in furs and white plastic. She came up to the cage and set a steaming bowl of soup before him through a low opening and smiled. Her form, her slender shape was so intriguing, inspiring as it were. A not unattractive face at all either, Acel thought. He'd thanked her profusely and tried to begin asking many questions at once, but she only giggled and shyly slipped away—with a backward glance that stirred life into Acel and he set at once to the good meaty stew, burning his mouth.

When he was nearly finished and feeling much more lively his observant cellmate chuckled behind him.

'Well, I guess maybe you get the picture now. In my part of the Dome the Area Governance sends out missionaries to the Outskirts with sort of the same strategy: soup for complicity. The most natural arrangement from any angle.'

'From any what?' Acel asked with his mouth full. The man's accent was sometimes hard to catch.

'You know, perspective, angle, from any point of view maybe it's a natural compromise. You're being set up, friend. Of course it's not a terrible arrangement, considering our position. I've just refused it myself for maybe 9 months now.' The man's eyes took a faraway look gazing over the cold desolate hills. 'I don't even know how much more I can handle. You see, these people, these people that dwell out here in this frozen wasteland, they're all sterile. They can't make babies—'

'Can't make *maybe's*, they have no—?'

'Babies, children! Listen. Their sexes are sterile out here beyond the Dome. Result of some kind of radioactive poison since the TransmuDream wars, you know. I don't know, they just can't. Once in a while, often as possible, they're able to capture some young stud lost from the Domes who *can* do it, and by God they put him to work in the nicest way. One of the young guys who'd accepted the whole deal and then had second thoughts explained it all to me after I'd refused the first few times. That poor devil was on the run in the night, and he made it by here. That young son wasn't around for long after that, maybe just a few days. They took him again on the third night, yes, now I recall it. That was curtains for him. It's human nature as I've seen it; the fatal dilemma of the eternal triangle: one loved by two. No one can stand it for long, not for free. Here the price is very high for your service. Too high for me. And of course they beat their women like dogs too—you'll see that. Seems that it's just not endured coolly by the male of their, uh, people. Now I guess maybe they're just waiting me out. You get the feeling they're hesitant to commit. What men wouldn't be, in their position? They'll wait you out too, I reckon. You're younger than me, right? I think so, maybe.'

'These people, these—' Acel waved his hand disgustedly at the white huts of the outlanders (a day ago he would've doubted their existence) 'these snow people are imprisoning me here to procreate them? What do they want—me to get with as many women as possible?' Acel was in fact considering the possibilities recalling the attractive woman who'd served him.

'It's shorter lived than you think. Even a friendly snake is not wanted in the house. Needed but not wanted. But maybe it's a way out. I've just got one already, see, in the Dome ... and I don't feel ... Really, for me, I just want to go home.' The man's voice dropped to an almost unintelligible murmur.

There was silence for a while, and Acel tried to put the picture together. He thought of his work, leaving it for this. He thought of the erotic famine he endured daily in the Domes, sustained only by TransmuCast fantasy. He thought of his mother waiting for him. He tried to imagine surviving in this icy climate day after day for years—how did they get this food, where did they clean or relieve themselves?

'I'm sorry, sir, I don't know your name ...'

'Maybe my last name would be easier to pronounce for you--Church. What's yours?'

'My first name's Acel.'

'That's a good name.'

'Most people laugh at it where I come from.'

'People express strategies to react to things that are different of course. Maybe that's what you're doing now. It's only my wife I miss, to be honest. Look, if I wasn't married in that damn Dome, I maybe *would* consider it the only way out here. Sometimes it seems a damn sight more friendly than ... territorial flatulence.'

Church let his voice trail off, but his last muttered words—if that's what hey were—made more sense than normal ones. Acel felt they both knew what he was referring to. Acel didn't want him to refer to it, because anywhere should've been better than his present predicament. But in the Domes there was a loneliness. The loneliness. The physical aching loneliness of every black bone in his body in the dark. Lying in his bed night after night with every bone in his body aching for physical contact, contact for which love is too small a word—which was always impossible, utterly impossible under the given circumstances. It was like death for so many nights after adolescence. But this is a ridiculous comparison. Acel was in perfect health, and that is what made it worse.

And this underscored the fact that played across the tightened corners of Church's thin mouth, that increasingly nobody ever talked about anything or anyone in the Domes, not about anything that really concerned anyone. Civilization under the Dome was on borrowed time, and everyone knew it deeper down than anything else in their lives. The human species had seen its salad days in an indulgent technology, TransmuDream, and now we were just coasting to a stop beneath its last farewell manifestation, the stagnant Dome. All the essential resources were all but run out, and markets were filled with unsatisfactory substitutes. Education was dead. TransmuCast advertising was the most effective ever designed by humanity—but it had done its work too well to save us. And deregulating the Outskirts, how much good would that do a passive stagnant populace? Even Acel could see this from his little nook in a forgotten library. Invention was contained; creativity was restrained; there were no imports; stagnant truths dominated the minds of our ponderous consumers. Things had changed drastically even in the time since he was a child and they used to get such luxuries as tiger's milk and bananas from the supermarket. But everyone avoided the painful truth so long as the TransmuCasts were ever more extreme entertainment. People got what they wanted in a fantasy. Things had run from opulence to mendacity in twenty years' time. How much time was left? How long before citizen strangled citizen for the last cup of clean water? Or would this last struggle simply manifest in a TransmuCast fantasy while the oblivious bodies sputtered and went out for good?

These were the kinds of questions that occupied a mind disengaged from TransmuCast for a half hour, Acel's mind. These were lonely thoughts. No one dared to mention the overwhelming fact that in the meantime, during the regularly unavoidable encounters in real life, everyone was simply begging for the scraps of love or personal attention they wrested from weak moments of others. Such an observation would not be politic and disturbs the machine-gun single-mindedness with which everyone constantly pursued what he or she felt to be their last chance at pleasure. Acel's own mind had often been on such things long hours at the library, reading with the madmen. That is, until he could get back to his computerized world. Yes, he was like the others, he conceded; just looking to occupy their painful unsatisfied waking hours with TransmuCast fantasy. Packaged but mutable dreamscapes where the results of all the pent up reality manifest immediate—in a suspended body charged with chemical manipulation. This is the version of life experience that was almost universal in the Dome. Somehow fortifying themselves for another barren day, until you could plunge again into the tactile products of the modern age. It was an illusion of self-sufficiency. And less and less these past few decades, could this endless mutual despair still manage to force persons into random life couplings and further disjointed unconnected families. How did this Church guy maintain himself at all in a marriage nowadays? With mad projects known as hobbies that are used to while away the time, playing like a child? Impossible, outside of TransmuCast; everything was impossible outside of TransmuCast. Family life was so devolved … into … a state Church described. This was recent life in the Domes. No way around it. Maybe their rich masters had it different, it was hard to imagine, even that.

'I met a man yesterday, or the day before,' Acel began. He felt impelled to describe all that had happened to him and longed for some reality with this nice man with the honest face. 'He said that I was an idiot, or an artist—he called it the same. I think he was a murderer … He said a lot about history and the stagnation of our Megalopolis. It seemed like it would die and be wiped out and die again …'

Acel clumsily stopped talking. Maybe he'd been wrong and they weren't considering the same realities at all. Church was gazing with heavy eyes over the snow covered hills, gazing far away at a life he would never have again and which he sorely missed. Somehow Acel felt he was slipt in, seeing through the inner man's eyes now. He was dreaming, watching the action blossom in the sepia colors of irresistible force. It was happening again, he knew, that fluid clairvoyant delirium. Such as it was on the mountain. The outside world was crazy, he was going crazy inside too! But it was the sweetest crazy. He was the man Church's life in a slow period of underwater bubbles. A large woman with warm and brutal eyes walking toward him, smiling indulgently. In a small blockhouse somewhere in the Dome. A curried saucy meal. Heaving sounds in a sweaty bed cloaked in darkness. His body's limbs were detaching dreamily, he had to stir toward continuity. A long grey sidewalk. A brilliant odor into blackness festooned with party lights.

'I stay alive because I deserve it,' Church was speaking again, staring sadly at the plastic floor of their cage. 'Maybe death is too good for me anyway, I don't know. But I do know that I must be punished by the appropriate hands, in my home, with my dear wife.'

Acel came out of it, curling away slowly in his tight sheet, wondering what sort of unfortunate beast he was locked up with now. How long could this residue teleportation craziness (what he called these inexplicable waves of intense empathy and clairvoyance) in his own head go on?

Church's voice showed he was in agony.

'It's ironic that I should learn as much as I now have about myself while I'm locked in a damn cage with no way to get out or back home and actually utilize my perspective to better someone's life, or my own. Just as one learns to live, life is taken away. Oh, how I would change the last twenty-four hours before I was kidnapped by these limp bastards! What I would give to change just ten seconds in that time if I couldn't change the whole time. In those few seconds I ruined everything. And then I was swept away! If only I'd left things the way they were before being captured, there may still be love rather than agony. I'm no better than an emotional marauder! Nine months ago I was a bigger fool than I am now. A selfish fool. Maybe it's better, who knows? There's nothing to distract me from this memory here. And I don't intend to hurl myself into pleasure and death to escape my memory either. Listen ...'

At this point Acel did not want to know whatever it was Church had done. It was frightening, but somehow Acel could not believe it was as bad as Church wanted to describe it. His features were so honest, square, his eyes so unbearably sincere that Acel felt there was even a modicum of warmth emanated in this awful place.

'My wife had gone to visit her mother, as she very often did, for several weeks at a time. It was because of her mother's TransmuCast, a beautiful big home theater type, they'd all watch together for days on end. Ours couldn't compare really. Our marriage was young. I was working heavily and sending most of the money to her for construction of the new house we were building next to her mother's. One evening after a difficult day—I was a Homeguardsman, you see, and spent all day controlling traffic near a business cone—'

'A business zone, oh well, I've seen ...' Acel offered.

'No, a business cone! Maybe you have them, maybe not, where you come from; everywhere does. I don't remember if you told me which Area. It's a machine anyway that dispenses credit to ID holders. Right. So I was beat. I stopped at a little beer bar for a drink. One was too much, twelve just wasn't enough! Nothing could stop me. Everything got out of control. Everything was lividly beautiful. Oh, what better than riding loaded onto the night with your glass full and your mind plunged into the sea of meaningful perception at last! This was nine months ago. I took one of those little waitresses home and what I did to her lasted all night long. Maybe that's a pleasant memory in this cage.' Church paused and looked down at his feet. His evident sorrow permeated Acel which he found it impossible not to pity. The pity was changed to stupefaction.

'And then I told her when she came back from the TransmuCast. That's the man I was. Wisdom may not come with age, but age certainly comes with wisdom.' Church observed wryly. 'Sometimes it seems as if there were two angels way, way up above the sky just talking together—maybe discussing at just what point in the night they're going to touch my brain. The most furious dreams become living reality. Madness.'

Acel did not like the direction of this conversation at all. He remembered being stuck with Venus, and the idea of enduring another lunatic in an actual cage forever face to face was impossible. This had to be resolved immediately. Acel might've had a sardonic character, but he was a soft-hearted man, and he would've liked to help Church's imaginary problems—his eyes told Acel only of wide open sincerity. Could there really be a black heart underneath such a gaze? What about Venus, could *he* have been true beneath his agony and rage? Acel thought of the last time he had seen Sir Venus, fighting for his life, for both of their lives. He couldn't understand the weird clairvoyance of those moments. It lived over and over in his mind. And the moments he had breathed in episodes of Church's life. Acel did not want to be elsewhere, unless it was back at his library desk this morning, and he did not want Church to confess anymore at all.

'Look, Church,' Acel gathered his strength. 'I don't need to hear this. I'm sorry about your unfortunate circumstances, your wife's addiction. But we have to put our heads together about how to get out of here now. I don't have much experience with women, I mean I've never been married like you. I'm sure it was, and is, difficult. But you can't just sit here confessing everything you know—what good does it do? You get it off your chest, make yourself feel better by making someone nearest you feel worse! Someone you say you love. Then you even get to play doctor with them after you've put your pain all right in their lap. It's selfish. If you can't do the time, don't do the crime, that's what they say, right? I mean, I don't have the experience, but ...'

Church lowered his head further and there was silence. Acel regretted his harsh words, but they had to come to the present, especially if what Church said about being used as an expendable stud was true! He didn't want to die. He didn't want to be swept into faraway visions. He wanted out of this cage.

'Maybe that's just your opinion.' Church muttered.

'Maybe it is!' Acel was exasperated. 'What's an opinion? I know what I need. I know what I want. I know who I am.'

'You're so confidant ... Many others, even in the Guard, tended to think of their lives as more of a search.'

'Look, Mr Church, ' Acel tried to calm himself. His eyes darted around outside the cell with a feeling they were wasting precious time. 'I told you I don't have all the answers and I don't have heaps of experience. But I've lived with myself for thirty years now! Shouldn't I have some experience by now knowing what I am?'

'You ask me to live a lie. Maybe what you propose is more selfish. Keeping your female in the dark—you call it protection. Your idea is summed up in the subjugation of another.'

'Selfishness? Subjugation?' Acel's curved mouth was spitting almost incoherently. He leaned forward and banged his head on the floor several times with his hands clawing the cold smooth plastic. Finally he spoke with difficulty, inhaling deeply with every other word. 'You're not the only one on Earth whose family is eaten up by TransmuCast! Makes you wonder why, how do we keep on at all? But no, it's too big, Nature's intent, propagation … is not what I would call *selfish*. Can you see where we are? Do you have eyes to see? This is a cage. You have informed me that we are marked for extermination after a short run of enforced breeding. *This* is subjugation, if you need an example!'

Church's voice assumed an officious tone, as if he were chuckling to himself. 'You admit to a love-hate relationship with someone whom you've admitted never meeting, since you never got married. You're stuck to a fantasy through a terrible combination of opposite feelings.   Maybe you enjoy the excitement.   Next you'll tell me that the TransmuCast everybody loves is a subjugation too.'

'I don't care! Do you understand this finally? I'm not going to sit here ruminating about ways that love, or my need to love, alright love then, ways that love is destroying my life!   And I'm not going to wait around in the name of *my* love, like you are, for someone else to destroy it for me in the name of *their* love! Maybe it won't be in a little idiosyncratic library, living with my parents, and eating the breakfasts I like while masturbating in a TransmuCast—but I will find a way to love and not be destroyed by it. And that's more than you're doing.'

Church had not raised his head and looked at Acel during all this conversation. It was as if he was not willing to admit another into the processes of his imprisoned mind.

Acel turned away and was scanning the small gate for any weakness in the hinges. He knew he had to do this alone, that this person had slipped beyond the point of being able to help himself.

'What I don't understand,' behind him Church spoke to Acel from under his brows. 'is that if I do something wrong or right or even random, and the Creator of the Universe, our Master, the Author of our lives knows about it already beforehand, how could I be free? How could I feel this way? And if I am not free, how could I be held guilty for anything I do?'

'Why shouldn't you be held accountable for your life, Church?' Acel said in the most bored voice possible. He didn't turn around.

'So I had no choice, did I? There are unknown causes, cosmic forces, influence of alien bodies ... I'm just part of the indescribable shape of the Multiverse fabric dancing in a concert with itself. I'm just a programmed TransmuCast, films for the Divine ...'

The conversation had not ceased as Acel wished; rather it had expanded grotesquely—nowhere including an escape plan.

'Look, Church, of course you have choice, at least over your attitude about things, you have as much choice as you can get. You make decisions. You live in Time. Our Master, as you say, lives in eternity and sees all the pictures and pages at all the same time. That doesn't mean your life is controlled by God, alright, just that it's known. Or maybe it *is* even controlled. But that doesn't matter to you. *You exist in Time.* You have to make all these decisions as they apply to you! Only other elements of Time will judge you, and I don't have the god-damn time to do that.'

'So you don't believe that God ever intervenes in our lives ...?'

Acel was silent for a long time. Something in Church's last question struck him to the bone. He dropped his eyes from the corners of the cage. He thought of the strange message he'd gotten that day (yesterday?) in the library, of Venus, all the books he'd read. The breathtaking coincidences of dreams and sudden dreamlike moments that feel so real to the memory and had made him yearn for answers all his life. He shuddered at his terror during Venus's fight in many places and how he'd seen it all in his mind or with his mind's eyes, and how he'd prayed for safety buried in the biting snow. And now somehow in this cage, but alive. He answered slowly, without argument in a tired voice.

'I hope so ... We all hope so. I don't know the ultimate nature of our Creator. Only some, I believe, sometimes.'

Church's eyes grew soft. He slowly smiled. 'I think the Master does intervene. There have been messengers and messages everywhere and there always will be. Thank you for our conversation. I enjoyed it.'

'Well, so did I,' Acel answered, and meant it. After a pause he smiled mischievously, 'And I hope our next one includes an escape plan.'

They smiled together.

Nothing was said after that, while Church merely gazed at Acel. Acel wondered if maybe he was waiting for an idea to spring up for their plan. Church certainly was idiosyncratic. Acel felt uncomfortable in the cold cage being stared at like that, so he looked away over the breathtaking white hills and snow carpeted trees glistening in the already setting sun and thought of the Dome. How far away was it? His home. He thought of its vast shape, which was described as ovular, with four short branching arms at equal angles. There were many images, real and imagined; everybody agreed it was a miracle of engineering and architecture, and that it could never be repeated. Apparently everyone who had designed it had taken this knowledge to the grave or to outer space or wherever the wise go. Why didn't Alien Advisors from other worlds ever come to visit Earth as they did in Acel's old book? Maybe that's what Venus is. No, he's too insane to be anything other than human, isn't he? Maybe aliens suffer too. Acel knew through his own studies that Cosmic Rangers had indeed designed the Dome with abilities inherited in nature's implosion during the TransmuDream collapse. Continents had shifted shape, so much matter had been displaced and elementally ruined and had become insubstantial. The Dome's megalopolis was supposed to spread over the last inhabitable area of the planet. But here, in these freezing mountains, were Outlanders like those rumored about in bars at the Outskirts. Drunk men talked a lot about anything. But here they were. Acel wondered how many people lived outside the Dome … and why did they bother? It didn't seem very comfortable. At least not in this cage.

'We speak the same language, but we have different accents,' he mentioned aloud.

'Yes, it must be the same all over,' Church speculated immediately, as if he had been watching him the whole time and waiting for a chance to speak. 'We can talk with these Outlanders too, did you know? Well, oh my goodness, how wonderful! Now maybe you'll find out.'

Acel became aware of a small white-draped head bobbing up and down just above the level of their cell's floor behind Church's lap. Suddenly he hoped it was the girl again who had served him. But in fact it was not a girl, unless one considers young a girl of about seventy-five. She smiled toothlessly at Church and stared at Acel with wide-open shy eyes.

'This is Pursula, my little friend.' Church gave her a wink. 'We share secrets together.'

Acel's spirits rose up into his throat. Surely this was their ticket out, this old grandmother would help them!

'Can she get the key for this cage door?' he whispered fiercely.

'Sh-sh-sh,' Church waved him off. 'She really shouldn't be here at all, you know. She just sneaks out for our little visits before bedtime—don't you, sweetheart?' The old woman nodded slowly. 'She is my steady confidant. We're both lonely and have had enough of society. She doesn't have the same opinions as you though …'

'Oh, for God's sake!' Acel exclaimed, convinced that this Church had simply gone mad out here. Everything was impossible and Acel felt again bereft of any reasonable way out. In a show of raging frustration Acel scooted around and stared ferociously at the growing night. He could hear the two secret friends giggling and sweet-talking behind him, his anger increasing in proportion to this terror; he was at the mercy of these filthy Outlanders, these snow-brained barbarians.

Night had fallen completely. The stars, bigger and clearer than he'd ever seen them, looked more tearlike than lonely travelers through a whistling emptiness forever. He did not notice the chatting had ceased behind him long ago. He was startled from his sorry reverie by Church's deep voice echoing a similar sadness.

'Well, my new friend, I don't know if I agree with everything you've said, though it was a perspective I guess maybe I needed to hear. But I don't think we'll have time to create an escape plan together just now.'

A door in the cage behind Acel swung open and strong hands took him by the legs.

'Remember what I told you, Acel! Refuse them! You'll be back!'

'Let go of me!' Acel struggled, but the Outlanders were too strong for him. Despite his clutching fingers Acel was dragged out of the cell across the hard ground. 'I want to stay in the cage! Wait!' he cried desperately but was ignored.

XIV

The electrical storm wasn't just a stroke of luck. It had blasted one of the demonical brothers, and Venus knew their characters well enough—once one of them was wounded the other would embrace his twin, cry like a baby, and go looking for their mama. They were too unswervingly devoted to each other to ever handle the agonies of a real world.

Venus sailed down through the excited mists and his feet landed squarely on the ground. He looked around at a desert. He figured he'd finally have at least one precious Gelatinous Cube in his possession before the Twins could ever return. They would never find it before he would. This young Acel Daniel felt like a sure thing somehow. Venus trusted his feelings. The words 'The Cube' evoked such reverence in his mind with himself; he desired it so completely as a panacea for all his frustrations and ills. His bowels moved plaintively with excitement. Venus had seen the power ages ago. He knew he wasn't the only one who'd love to have the Cubes, but he was the best. He had eliminated much of the competition. Venus thought proudly over his growing army of little sons. The Cubes could help them grow. Venus squeezed his eyebrows together. He wasn't sure what the genuine Cubes were composed of. His own experiment had yielded him a barely adequate receptor, and that was all. It was impossible to transmit anything with it, and not only that, it cast a field of interference that interrupted most other transmissions, which meant that he was actually receiving less than he should have.

Venus pounded his fists together. 'Not for long! Now! Did I leave that runt in the sand or in the snow?'

He'd been obsessed with perfecting his own experiment for so long. For eighty-seven years he'd used the brainstems of the most intelligent and resourceful men in the Domes, in the Outskirts, the Outlands. He'd rigged a sort of electrified soup after the models he'd been exposed to—and it had really worked up to a point. Of course he had always interrogated his subjects first, just as he planned to do with Acel. The extraordinary possibility of recollection from a previous life was the idea that had driven his obsession. Venus was convinced that the most primitive sections of the brain must somehow contain impressions formed in an earlier life, a previous incarnation. How memory could pass between two different biological entities occupying different time-space coordinates, was a process for which he had no name, nor clear conception of. He was not sure if a person was actually existing in infinite places already during a universe in eternity, while their time-bound minds merely had to know these living aspects one by one in lives, like one being with many souls; or if an essential vibration was emanated at death, what one might call a released spirit, that found its way through laws of attraction to a new home across the universe in an appropriate fetus's developing brain, influencing that new life forever, in fact becoming it, and so on through lives. Venus played with the logic constantly. The later theory was his favorite because it was practical. Brainstems were inherited batteries of collectable transmittable energy. There was some primal formation in them that was sensitive to the wavelike emanations released upon death, emissions small enough to move faster than time. A new fetal formation attracted the nano vibration, captured it, and grew along according to it, until it's own end and the soul was scattered again. Inside the fresh brainstem, in a maddening nest of DNA introns, the quantum vessel was smaller than atoms, more delicate than vacuum, but hungrier than the sun. It was the honeycombed wick of a well-traveled spark—Who knows how long it had developed, what it had seen, and how it began? If Venus could ever draw these impressions together into one viable congruous memory, death on this wasted planet would loose its disgrace and its sting.

And yet his own invention *had* worked to a certain degree—he was able to receive collective signals, messages from deep patterns below the surface life of the world, from a deeper more essential realm.

Venus's willingness long ago to experiment with human subjects here brought him into conflict with the authorities who had counted him as missing in action soon after his memorandum was refused. This was also very soon after the present Domes were erected, a project he'd assisted with. Venus had served as a sapper with the Cosmic Rangers. He had been a non-commissioned officer who had never taken authority well. Although daring, which accounted for his rise within the lower ranks, he had been reprimanded and punished severely several times for insubordination and neglection of duty. There was no love lost between his officers and himself, and his disappearance was not sorely missed. In any event, the Cosmic Rangers had survived mutating forms and manifestations of numerous implosion/explosions in many dangerous engagements, and an enlisted man's casualty while furloughing on his home planet was not an extraordinary case. Rangers have been torn apart by nostalgia and duty while an entire planet implodes, and were never seen again. His commanding officer, a capable man named Bunder (Mjr B. A. CR Sct Cav. 444A87A, to present time), in this case shrugged his shoulders and said, 'To hell with him at last.' Then he made a mental note to ban furloughs on any Ranger's home planet—a memo that was never quite taken up due to obvious restrictions on certain species' psyches.

[NB *Although Venus's identity is not mentioned, there is a record of Mjr Bunder's repetition of these circumstances in his relevant file of the time.*]

Although Venus had experience with engineering he certainly had been able to get little information regarding the construction of the first Gelatinous Cubes on Earth, the site of their invention before Venus's birth. He had no idea where they were, and as we know, they had never been reproduced. Samples of them after TransmuDream had been taken far and wide but these had had short duration and the original athanors' location was a top secret subject. But Venus had no doubt they were still being used up to the time of the reconstruction of the Dome. The Device he used now, his own mimicry of what he'd learned about the Cubes, did more than absorb vague esoteric transmissions and locate extraordinarily aware humans (men for their brain material and women for his towers). And it had done more than grant the man with a surplus of unnatural strength and powers of diabolical illusion. It also received particles of classified TransmuCasts in the slough, from an deeper source—enough to lead him to believe the Cubes on his planet not only were *still* being used now, but that a larger operation was afoot which would bring those Cubes into his direct revelation. Venus meant to intercept it. In his mind he anticipated an archangelic double penetration begun from every angle of the enthused membrane between worlds. Venus felt sure that Acel Daniel was a descendent of this plan and was a key to Venus's very future. It was in Acel's brain and Venus would have it one way or another—it would crown his machine. Venus wanted one of those Gelatinous Cubes more than anything else life had ever promised to offer. An empire of his own and a legend of petty revenges teemed cornucopia in his harried proud mind, which still felt the final terror of punishment for his desertion from the service. He vowed he would change things. His strange and inferior Device still nourished many of the various powers and attributes a Ranger might have, while corrupting his mind.

And now, with his big red mouth hanging open, Venus knew he had more work to do. He became aware of something very disturbing to him far away ... A swelling unease, as one feels when another is watching the back of one's head and the hair starts to lift up.

'Durn, burn it!' he shouted. With a glance toward the snow-covered peaks far to the south where he'd decided he'd left Acel, he leapt in the opposite direction.

Then with a fiery gasp he pulled up short and with his whole spirit gazed to the east, toward his beloved towers. They hung like silky needles of obsidian against a distant dream plain of ash in a puff of smoke—amidst his scorched history the ripening fruit of his ambition. In a powerful moment his mind was in the past, submerged in the happiest times of his life. Years before, entering chamber after blessed chamber; surrounded in devoted little girls, happy rays of sunshine beaming from individual delicate stars, each relying on himself alone for life and adopted fatherhood. He'd kept them often in common rooms at that age: little girls animate each other. He'd taught them to. But now, what were the secrets that he sensed glide between them like the shadow of a passing bird? What was it in the back of their princess's mind, his natural princess?—they all were, but somehow his precious Diona was more so. This concern had exacerbated the harried cast thrown over his life by his own ambition and unsettled his certainties.

But there it was again—the awareness creeping over him of some burning broiling thing in his world. With the aid of his arcane Device Venus could sense with discomfort the turmoil and steady pour of any human mind's creativity within range as he roamed the globe. And when he did, their fates were not various. Venus was a jealous godling wherever he roamed.

'Fools! The fools on this planet! However could someone such as me be descended from them? It's a miracle my dear shortlived parents ever survived many forms at all ... Rangers ... Did I really come from here?' Venus was tossing his head melodramatically as he flew rapidly through the air. 'How can I get a job done with so many of these greedy idiots searching for power they don't understand? Three this year! Why are they springing up like crazy lately? Oxnard, Acel, and who's this? Ah, I feel them! Why don't they just *stop*? No, I don't want them to. I need them, it is crucial now. Well, little Acel, your namby-pamby brain will just have to wait, yes it will!'

It did not take long for Venus to be back deep inside the nearest Area of the Dome, an Area he had not been to in many years. But he had become aware of some scant trace of reflective high intelligence once again, and that was something he must have for his own. Venus crept through the darkening streets. He was drawn to a house; step by step he felt the magnetism compel him. The house was old, large, surrounded by a very wide weedy yard, in a loose row of other dilapidated old places just like it. Or so it seemed from the outside.

Night had fallen in the Dome.

In back of the old house was a ramshackle warehouse built from sheets of tin. Venus drew near it with gathering fury. There were no windows or door he could see; it seemed to open into the back of the house through a clumsy passage. Now Venus did not live in any part of the Domes but he knew this was not normal at all. Venus stalked around it like a lion over a fresh kill. 'What is this? What is this?' he kept muttering between snorts of his huge nostrils. Putting his fingers between a seam in the tin sheets he tore open one of the thin walls of the warehouse. It peeled away with a shriek and hung drooping and quivering. A weak light fell over him from inside. Venus craned his head in and a grimace of surprise and disgust possessed his face.

'What is this? A travesty!'

Inside the warehouse under a large dim lamp a bizarre vehicle lay in a state of obvious near-completion. Its body was composed of a long bus, one of those used for mass transit within Areas of the Dome. But its entire length was covered over with a hard metal Venus had rarely seen, and not for a long while. It was like the TransmuFormed crystal of the Dome but opaque, though he couldn't recall what the engineers had ever used to do with this particular alloy. There was so much going on at that time that Venus didn't have the time for. Venus could not think of how it got here, and it enraged him. Mouth gaping, he stared at one part and then another. Short winglike projections protruded at intervals down its sides and back. The rear of this apparent rocketship was crowded with heavy exhaust pipes from which vast quantities of energy could be thrust out, impelling the crazy machine to God knows where.

A light went on in the house above and a window opened.

'Who's out there?' a voice boomed down across the yard. Venus did not respond or seem to notice. He remained fixed on the obscene creation inside the warehouse, face twitching with bewildered revulsion.

'I said, You! Get away from there!' the voice boomed again accompanied by the heavy slide-click of a shotgun cock.

At last Venus turned, as if stunned. 'Where did you get that material?' he asked quietly.

'I'll blast you! Get away from here!' the man above him shouted again, but suddenly seemed to think better of it and added, 'Haven't you ever seen a steel mill before, you idiot? This is a factory. You're on private property. Now get out of here or I'll blast you for trespassing!'

Venus's jaw trembled, but his voice couldn't have sounded more at ease. 'Relax, old man, I was just looking for something to eat. I guess a job would do me, if you got anything around here ...' Venus emerged into the light shed from the window. The man saw a juvenile delinquent, thin and wasted.

'Well, there's nothing around here, so get on with you!'

'You're not very friendly.'

'I'm warning you!'

Venus shrugged and walked away in the dark, the shotgun muzzle following his every step.

XV

When the old man was satisfied that punk kid had really gone he closed the window and turned back downstairs into his old kitchen. He felt a little hungry. That excitement must have taken a lot of energy out of him. But he knew he shouldn't eat anything so late as it bothered his stomach once he lay down to sleep, like bile coming up. 'Maybe I'll smoke.' That was something else he knew he shouldn't do at anytime, but did anyway at night.

He leaned the shotgun in the corner by the sink and found the cigarets in a drawer. He often sat at his old mica kitchen table, smoked and thought things out. Sometimes he sketched his ideas with a pencil on blank paper usually lying there after his habit. But as paper had become more expensive he used the wall above the table. This was very unpopular with his sister, whom he shared this house with. But as pencils too became increased in price he was forced to rely on frustrating little children's crayons to express himself. Yet his meager work had gone on. He never played TransmuCast, and in fact was one of the few people alive in the Dome without a connection. He was out of the circuit.

His name was Rudolf Kingsburg. He had of course never been a Cosmic Ranger and had never known anyone who had, not to his knowledge. He didn't know anyone who had known anyone who had either, and he didn't like weird conceptions about such things. These were the kinds of thoughts Rudolf Kingsburg's personality took repose upon with relish. And yet, for many decades of years he had been a doting caretaker to one of the strangest post-TransmuDream inventions built by human hands, freshly from those old devastating days. These kinds of contradictions are central to most human behavior, and literally hordes of people resemble Rudolf Kingsburg in this, whatever the object (though very rarely something so arcane), a simultaneous defense and indulgence of something not really understood; it always has a doting aspect. This position of caretaker had been bequeathed to Rudolf Kingsburg and he accepted it willingly; he had loved those who secretly created that machine in his warehouse. They were two brothers, automobile mechanics employed by the Dome for the mass transit lines. They used to spend their spare time building such dangerous contraptions as motorized gliders or electric wheelchairs—often dreaming of a time when the Outskirts would be deregulated and they could explore the wild with one of these haphazard vehicles, but that never happened in their lifetimes. Owing to a very singular event, their own eccentric ideas flourished when they'd found a huge supply of a strange metal, in flexible sheets beneath Rudolf Kingsburg's struggling garden many years ago. It had obviously been a leftover from the Dome's very construction, and they did not report it. Instead they decided to use it for the greatest invention they could think of, and which Rudolf Kingsburg, then and now, worshipped. These two ingenious brothers had sadly passed on in a mysterious accident far from home that it hurt him to think about. So now he cleaned their legacy, he maintained it, and more so lately, did everything he could to finish it in his own way after his idols.

The old caretaker lit up and congratulated himself on his treatment of that punk. As he did so, his cat strolled into the room, a mostly cream colored creature with umber face, nose and ears—a breed that was still called Siamese though Siam had long ago refused to exist. The cat was called Radar because it spent most of its time, when it wasn't out chasing pussies, poised watching a space slightly aside of Rudolf's body. Rudolf Kingsburg lived with this old cat and his sister, Victoria, who was asleep in her room. They were both widowed, but had never had children. These circumstances had brought his sister to stay with him now for years, although she was usually extraordinarily bored without the

TransmuCast that Rudolf didn't allow in his house—in fact she always lied to anyone she knew and said they did have it. But family was the steadfast cord in the storm.

Rudolf Kingsburg watched a fat cockroach wing from nowhere to collide in a dark corner of the hall across from him and hurry down to the floor. 'God damn it,' he thought and leaving his cigaret put his had on the shotgun, his first thought to smash the vermin with its butt. In half a second he'd changed his mind about this choice of weapon, but what he saw next convinced him to stay where was with his had still on it.

A figure appeared in the passage and was already silently emerging from the shadow.

'Who the hell are you?' Rudolf Kingsburg demanded lifting his gun to the ready at his hip. But slowly his face became puzzled.

The man standing before him was a little less in years than himself, but the face that had just come into the light bore such resemblance to the kid he had just chased away that he thought they must be the same person, that maybe he hadn't seen this man properly in the dark down in the yard and had thought he was a kid. However this did not change his opinion, which was also irritated by the fact that now his nightly cigaret was burning away without him.

'Where did that metal come from?' Venus ignored his demands.

'None of your god damned business. You've got five seconds to clear out of this house and three are already gone.'

'Now take it easy, ha ha! It's a good thing we met when we did!' Venus smiled and began smoothly, rubbing his hands down the length of a finely made suit which wove itself down to expensive and fashionable shoes; his hair became suave. A blue steam rose from his body. 'I've had to traipse all over this Area looking for any old scraps of this stuff, since everyone's being paid so well who has come across any of it—well, the government's got to have what it needs to repair the Dome, of course. You throw in that old mill out there too and I'll take care of the whole bill right now for you, and have the whole supply carted away before morning. Anyway, I'm about beat and I'm looking to get back to my hotel, so I'm just uh … dying to settle this with you here first.'

Venus did not step but rather hovered slightly into the room, his eye fixed with indiscernible agitation on the shotgun's bore. This was the second time this evening that little black hole had been pointed at him.

'I'm not the kind of man to be taken in by fast talking and I don't like the fact that you have come in without knocking at the front door like normal people. Besides it's too late for visitors. And, we *haven't* met.'

Rudolf raised the gun menacingly. Venus looked at it with distaste. He knew himself to be very strong and very fast, but a point blank range 12 gauge would injure him extremely inconveniently before he could neutralize its wielder. Deception and distraction should serve his purposes. Sometimes the best deception is the truth delivered in strategic doses.

'Your race submits to me easily,' he stated. A wisp of smoke climbed up from one of his brow.

The men looked each other in the eye. Like two armies massed against each other in the break of dawn. The eye of Venus shown like a blue star, with hideous glittering flames; it was like a hole in the void, a void inside of it. But brown-iris'd Rudolf did not back down.

'You might be the Devil himself, I'm not selling you that metal or that ship— that mill,' Rudolf Kingsburg caught himself in low fury. 'You just go on back to your bosses and tell them I don't want none, or go look somewhere else.'

'A ship, is it? A starship! Is that what you think you'll do?' Venus laughed insistently. He believed he'd found the advantage he was looking for. He wanted to mock this ambition, and tear it open, tear it asunder, expose this insolent organism to the pink shame of its naked old mushroom cells, its stringy feeble tenderness doing what is repulsive and what is called pathetic when it had felt shame as he had.

'Oh, yes, I sympathize with your amazing aspirations. Your *scientific pursuit*.' Venus mocked him.

'But I didn't ... That mill's none of your ...'

'But how could I let you go on in your search, knowing that someone like you, someone so wonderfully beautifully intelligent, with a brain, ah yes, a brain one could lust after! By God, look at that contraption out there in your garage! That's the best you can do?'

'Well, maybe the jig is up. Here's my cards on the table. But I didn't build it, and you don't work for no government.'

Venus ignored him. He moved his arms in oratory gestures. 'Someone like you might possibly even discover the wonderful Cube before me, couldn't you? Is it not possible? I've devoted my life for 80 years to this, ever since I'd decided to work only for myself. I remember when the idea first came to me.' Venus leaned back in reminiscence, raising his hand softly above him. 'What was I then? Nothing. Like you. A namby-pampy peon. Enduring punishments for my self-expression. Caged with a heart as big as a lion's. Screaming myself to sleep. And then, one night in the regimental stockade, alone with the weak moonlight peering through the bars ... I think that time I'd organized a platoon for hunting, to put some variety on our table in the evening." Venus grinned like a naughty schoolboy proud of his classroom exploits. "There were still quite a few weird species on Earth then and rebuilding these Domes was a gruesome bore ...

Maintaining the colony was, too. That was all before those durned darned hordes of reptilian ...' Venus spat out incoherent words while red patches inflamed his cheeks. At last his eyes cooled to a terrible grey. 'Ah! I don't want to go on about that war. Protecting our species. We were all different men then, naïve, weak. The present ruling class in these Domes doesn't make it legal to explain how the Domes were built, does it? At the time after the war there was the theory of humane security. It was argued that the species would thrive if they weren't educated to the fact of recent beginnings following total devastation. A false security was better than none. But look at them now. They produce very little for themselves. The process will be long, if they don't die out first.'

Venus paced in a circle. 'So I thought of using the knowledge of the past, all our past! It must be trapped inside of us somehow. The idea came to me with the lucidity of waking in a pure clear summer morning. Silence and surety all around. You know when something is true. Like one's own heartbeat. It was as if God had spoken to me in the night. I just had to find a way to extract the knowledge from the body. I believe there are nano-sized conductors patterned in the brain. They're possessed by quantum waves released at death. They produce the waves, they release the waves! The waves for a moment are almost everywhere at once until trapped again into a life shape and circumstance most resembling the previous. One complete life most resembling another in eternity. The waves are not in Time, not in life, really, you see? At conception this is enough to enter and influence, to possess, to trap the quantum awareness into another life, with its old wave system and reestablishing its pattern! Do you see? I am the master of the brainwaves! I am the genius of immortality! Once I have that Cube, the universe will be free from Death forever!'

Venus's face had grown bright red now, his fists clinched in the sky. But Rudolf Kingsburg did not lower his shotgun, though he was unnerved to say the least.

Suddenly there was a form in the hall. Rudolf's sister had woken up with the noise.

'Rudy, has someone come over—?' she caught herself as she came up behind Venus's massive back in the dark little hall.

The cat screamed from some hiding place. In a desperate lunge Venus grabbed for the woman. She was slipping under his arms when their ears were slapped with the shotgun's blast. A hail of dust filled the kitchen. Venus had leapt into the ceiling, doing as much damage there as the gun had done to the jamb. He landed on all fours, staring up again at that hated little black muzzle. The sour stench of sulfur hung between them.

Rudolf's sister stood behind him, shaking, trying not to cry. Radar purred around her leg.

'Who is that, Rudolf?' she cried.

'Shut your pie hole, Victoria. This man is probably going to die!'

Venus's mind was working faster than perhaps it ever had. His peripheral vision shot out to every corner of the devastated room. He sensed there was still some hesitation in the old man. He was not a killer. He was a warm hearted indulgent old creature ...

'You didn't build that starship.'

'He didn't! What do you want from us?'

'Shut up, Victoria!'

'I can fly it,' Venus said simply and stared back at Rudolf Kingsburg. He was bluffing, but he thought he had finally found the niche, the finger hold that would drag his quarry to him. And he just might be able to fly it, all the same—that would be something on his side no matter what.

'Look, you,' Rudolf Kingsburg was loathe to believe this maniacal claim. 'I don't know about all you've said. It sounds, it sounds bizarre. I don't think young men should get involved in philosophy and poetry and all that. You ought to work, and work hard—you'll find out what life's about. Later you can study science, and build something useful. But now look at you. You're violent—'

'I'm not a young man anymore. You don't know how long it's taken me, how long,' Venus began in pitiful tone.

'Oh, get him out of here, Rudy, he's crazy!' Rudolf's sister picked up the cat and backed away toward the sink.

'Be quiet, Victoria, God damn it. I'll handle this. He's not the first self-pitying punk I've seen in my day. When I was young I wasted probably ten years drinking and carrying on, myself. And the things I remember I used to say, I don't know how my brains were screwed into my head at all. I admit it. Now you just look what happens when you get older but you haven't changed your ways. Mister, you're a wreck. You talk crap. And I got nothing you want here. You say you can fly that, that *beautiful creation*. I doubt you could ride a bicycle.'

'Now you listen!' Venus remained on the floor, his clothes ragged with an air of respectability neglected through hard times. 'I'm older even than I look. I've seen things neither one of you can think of. I've seen the Earth in a state of dying beauty. It was my duty to observe, in those days. Supine, still flamboyant, a goddess is what your home was. Delicate were her creatures with bones of milk and intentions harder than steel. Like virgin was so much of her unrevealed surfaces, below the sea, betwixt the mountains' livid roots. Humans, her favorite children. With dignity she took the blows your ungrateful impatient race unleashed through a technology that made the minds of angels weep!'

'He's crazy, Rudy!'

'I don't know about that old stuff, nobody does.'

'I know you don't! How could you? You are children, children of the Dome I built with my own two hands and those of my men. And yet … and yet,' Venus's lips began working beyond his own control, spitting. 'You try to kill me, me! Have I ever turned my nose up at your hospitality? Have I ever forgotten to say Thank You? Have I ever plotted behind your back when you've allowed me my freedom and security and safety, and given me the chance to flourish with an independent love while you kept the devils off my back for me? Have I ever bitten your hand while it was feeding me? Nyooooh! So why do you do it to me?'

'Oh my God, Rudy, he's sick! He has a mind problem. Can't you see?' Victoria clutched at her brother's sleeve, but he ignored her.

'Where do you come from?' Rudolf asked menacingly. He had to keep up the front. He realized he was beyond his depth with this dangerous man, but that reminded him of something else, something sweet and distant, the delight he used to feel listening to the geniuses who built the craft out in his warehouse. They had skills, imagination; they talked in circles around his brain which marveled at the impressions that were granted him just through listening. He had never opened his mind to any others. Those two were his guides, his teachers; they were his secret and he cherished their memory as he now cherished and maintained their legacy.

'What does it matter to you now?' Venus howled. 'I risked my blood fighting the reptilian minions of the discarded Twins' idiocy—for your species. The attack came just when we thought your lives would be secure in a nearly complete Dome. Did you care? *Nyoooh.* Did my *superiors*—I use the word in massive mockery—did they care the slightest bit? *Nyoooh.* I wasn't granted permission to use one iota of what my vast field experience had shown me. The facts that I painstakingly dragged out of the universe with my bare fingers!' Venus remained on the floor, fondling the air with pulsing claws. 'The most intense mystery of mortality is within my grasp! Why couldn't they understand me? Why is it obstacle after obstacle? Well, I have my pride left and I will never forgive them! Why are my messages an obstacle rather than an enlightenment?'

Rudolf Kingsburg and his sister stood looking down at this distraught humanoid being, as one might look at an extremely ill leopard in a cage—in this case, at gunpoint. What had begun in Venus as an intention to deceive and manipulate had twisted into a terrible desire to be appreciated. There is a reaction of conceit among the few species with reflective consciousness in this universe whereby certain urges of oneself are detested in order to gain distance from others of them. One result is a periodic inner collapse. Although Venus's origins are unclear, he was obviously liable to this tendency.

'Let me fly your machine!' he demanded and groveled like a madman grasping for the one idea of salvation. 'You'll see how good a pilot I am!'

Victoria stared at her brother. 'You're not going to give him a chance, are you? I've always had more common sense than you and you know it. He's a stranger, Rudy. You love that machine, whether you can fly it or not—'

'Enough!' Rudolf shouted. She had pricked his pride in the place he abhorred the most. This did not escape Venus.

'Yes, but *I* can fly it! I was educated with the Rangers to do that very thing. We'll fly together, Rudy. We'll take her for a spin. Then we'll come back. We can become famous men, or we can do it in secret—you give the word.'

'Rudy!'

'Let's go down and check it out,' Rudolf relented. He could not decide if he was being betrayed or if the dream he most cherished was opening like a miraculous blossom beneath his feet. No one had ever suggested this, no one else even knew about his cherished pet hobby except his sister who had tolerated a lifetime of his eccentricity. And this could be a chance to prove Victoria's sharp tongue wrong about it all these years.

Venus pranced to his feet like a happy dog. 'Yes! Yes! It's always been one idea, one idea that has motivated me: *consciousness!*'

'Don't do anything stu—' Rudolf's words were cut off in stupefaction as the orangutangian stranger leapt up, flung open the nearest window and dove outside. He struck the ground in a rolling somersault that ended near the opened warehouse flap.

Rudolf and Victoria stood looking down in a kind of shock with their mouths fallen open.

Long seconds passed after Venus had gone into the Warehouse. Finally Rudolf roused himself with concern to get down there.

'Smoking again, I see.' Victoria had already edged around the kitchen and was considering how to clean up and forget the men's madness.

Suddenly the night was ripped by a scream from down in the yard followed by abominable curses and cussing. With certainty Rudolf Kingsburg thought of the Homeguard and if his shotgun hadn't brought them around this screaming nonsense would. His neighbors of course, to hell with them, they were all plugged into the TransmuDream. Still Rudolf thought it would be prudent to tell the maniac to keep it down—or maybe just to leave altogether would really be the best idea after all. He leaned back to the window.

He was down there alright, enraged again, pointing one finger first at Rudolf then at the warehouse then at Rudolf again.

'Where's the durn burned fuel?'

Rudolf leaned out. He was hoping that Victoria wasn't hearing this. She came over and stood near the window, very alert.

'Well, I'll come down and we'll talk about it—I'll explain it—' he began sheepishly.

'Why don't you just tell him you don't have any and you don't know what it uses anyway so just go away?' Victoria was sick and tired of all of it.

Rudolf's face turned beet red in the kitchen light. Venus had heard her and understood.

''What's that? No fuel? Why you foolish little man! You absurd pathetic apostle! You waste my time. Day in and day out maintenancing a mysterious machine that you don't understand and can't operate. Now I see you for what you are. You tried to deceive me! How can I blast off this rock with this piece of junk? This, *I had thought*, would have been a perfect introduction to your fine eggbrained Dome government—for both of us, Rudy! The Conscience of the Dome! What a ridiculous appellation they have. Moral weaklings, all humans! Have I ever deceived *you* with promises I can't fulfill? ...'

Rudolf was too offended to remember he still carried his shotgun; he was too mortified to remember anything and stood paralyzed staring down at his tormentor. His sister leaned out and shouted at Venus.

'You're the one who should be ashamed! You don't work for the government. You're a liar, and I see you wanted to steal the thing my brother's been working on his whole life for your own selfish purpose. I am so disgusted in you I want you to leave our property right now!'

Instead of the mocking laugh Venus had instantaneously reserved for her, his mouth clamped shut. It was a woman's voice. No, he had heard many in his unnaturally long career, so many girls for years filling the chambers of his needle towers with the sighs of destiny. Those halcyon years, they were his salad days, when he'd been carrying out his plan of creating his own flesh and blood empire among the most beautiful and intelligent of the human race. So many sweet memories for which he'd become a willing donkey of pleasure. Riding to his destiny as an emperor should.

For a wistful moment he gazed upward at Victoria's handsome and resentful countenance. Then his world was plunged into agony. The presentimental clairvoyance that transfixed him so often since his experiments with the brain matter—the intuitions that had led him here, or to Acel Daniel, or to Renegades and brains in every corner of the globe—coming over him it magnetized his senses once again. There were his needles on the black plain. There was one tower vacant again that should never be so, a torn cloth rope of yellow silk hanging from its slit window halfway down—impossible for a human girl!

'But she, oh my goddess, so much more than human!'

Venus clutched the red hair on the sides of his head and stumbled around like a drunk man about to pass out.

'No, no, no—I would give everything. Everything that should be mine! Just as I am about to rise to glory, this … Fate! I should be in your number, you on high, yoou, yooouu, as I used to be. But I obstacle, I impede, you don't communicate the secrets to me! This will not be my exile forever. A world I helped to build. Why can't I triumph here? Come back, don't leave so soon, come back!'

To say that Rudolf Kingsburg and his sister Victoria were now glad to see this maniac run off faster than they had ever seen anyone run before would be accurate. They looked at each other a few moments in the window frame. However many sleepless nights were to follow. The meaning of the world had torn open a little, from a quaint and compulsive little mystery into a larger more unsettling one. At times Rudolf Kingsburg wished he could hide his vestigial starship away, far away. At other times he wished that a good force, someone powerful and heroic from the old days of the Cosmic Rangers would come and thank him for his efforts and reward him and do battle with that bad maniac and destroy him with the starship that Rudolf had in his small way helped to maintain. That would be reward enough.

Eventually, Rudolf just got on as he had before (though perhaps with an increased sense of importance). Oddly enough, his sister never much mentioned this incident which he was sure she'd go on about nagging forever. Rudolf kept his dreams to himself too.

[I refer to my old reports, your Excellency, regarding this 'Venus' (CHTHNK 109.b [personnel] and REDOME 69a.b.f). The man is an idiot, your Excellency. Review the previewing disciplinary actions, if he is the same man, which Rice's report seems to indicate. Investigations should be brought at once to negotiate his actuality as a representative of accepted humanity, an archaic throwback, a cryptozoid, or perhaps something not quite human (see Krystal Elioud as earlier referenced). I believe that at one time His Excellency the Minister Haniel was interested in the Venus case, or am I mistaken?—Mjr Bunder]

XVI

Through a rainbow of fields and plains she ran like the wind. Many weathers changed about her like glittering dreams as she ran like she had never known running before. When Diona was a child, ah yes, she was strong and fast. And though womanhood had come upon her small frame with irregular suddenness, adult size now provided her with strength she could not have expected living in the narrow tip of a needle-like tower.

Like so many natural human events that have lain not dormant at all but growing, growing like an underwater flood against a material stricture, Diona's strength was fated to break through at what was a simple decision toward freedom.

'Run, run, baby, run,' she kept saying to herself.

Neither did she eat nor drink for a period far longer than normal human expression is capable of. Her body was in a stasis while it moved according to her will, without complaint. Over snows, rivers and deserts, in a direction judged at whim—through long captivity Diona had earned this desire. Certain natural rights may even be accumulated through long and painful experience—and they are not typically judged from a moral standpoint. To run criss-cross for forty days and nights over a great lobe of Earth's hemisphere is nothing but artistic.

Soon enough she ran to the places that the humble denizens of the Dome could no longer graph, nor do more than plot, were they interested; they weren't. This report should be understandable not only to the sentience in our Council. As the human intelligence in our Dome was erected on the once-conserved resources of fair Earth, resources bled away without renourishment. On the opposite side of our world lay refuse and toxic debris. A stench of collected rejection and displacement, run amok with its own weirdish nature, or what might pass for nature. There was the source of fungus, excrescence, irritating bacteria. Remnants of the explicably cruel reptilian parasite that evolved like men from short time to short time in malicious hordes under the masters of an overthrown world. Their progenitors were destroyed in episodes for which war is too small a word. Those indirectly responsible for their machinelike appearance and so much intimate destruction, the diachrome Twin Dukes, were hurled to our ephemeral material world in their sin, ruing the memories of a more essential realm of dense and sensitive matter struck away from their four creeping hands and wandering tongues. Once a Watcher of the oldest order, the Twins' mother had long ago abandoned them for one of the strangest love affairs of Cosmic history—a greenhorn Ranger had fled with her to places unknown in a new life. But she is known for many strange loves, and it was not the first time humanity's memory was scorched with her passion: one of the earliest documented humans in our records had even tried her for a wife before her unfaithfulness disgusted him. Such is her story. Her next famous lover, the demonic criminal father of those Twins (I feel no need to inscribe his name here) was captured on a hideous bed in hideously sweet mineral orgasm, in Egypt, as you well remember, and now fumes in supernatural irons beneath the core of the universe. But these were the kinds of forbidden intercourses that produced those whom humans at once celebrate and fear. Especially when these creatures are born among us, within our own warm bodies.

Diona stood watching a hotpink river flow. Some strange settlement spread on the opposite bank, of an uncharted populace. A feeling of female adult ambition flooded her smooth yearning limbs, such as she'd known only more vaguely as a child.

But now an era in Diona's existence passes out of the realm of this report. There is even knowledge unrecoverable after backtracking through the gelatinous nano logs that were stored in the mysterious Cubes—tedious chore. Consider it possible that at this time her blossoming existence went through indecipherable stages. Or went back through them. For a sizeable dollop of human civilization, 100,000 years long, had never taken place in her collective memory as it had in Acel Daniel's. Art, as expressed for example in her wild torrential flight, art for art's sake had never been tempered for any other purpose. Power craved itself. Desire desires desire. No cessation. No cessation of the tornado of anguish. That is to say, she who was born from the Nephilimic agent known as Krystal Elioud (PAT) had mind patterns that had never been human, but occurred earlier, elsewhere, above even the Cosmic Rangers, and she was now loose upon the face of the Earth.

XVII

What is known is that sometime within those forty days the one called Venus (whose record is mysteriously incomplete) arrived at the forbidding towers that he built with his own hands. There he encountered the greatest despair of his life: one of his towers, his favorite and most cherished, was vacant. A knotted rope of silken sheets hung down uselessly.

Like a drunk man he stumbled toward it and embraced it with his head leaning and pressed against it. It seemed to him that life was very cruel. Not one of his ambitions had been fully realized; every one of his efforts was an abortion. And that's all it would ever amount to, a disgusting goulash of severed attempts—that's all a disembodied soul could be left staring at when life was finally over. It was criminal really to Venus's mind that such a state of affairs could be allowed to exist. And his own natural demise at the end of an unnaturally prolonged life he regarded as outright murder. The blame as usual he assigned to the authorities that had at more than one time imprisoned him. They were the ones responsible for the inefficacies of his mimicking invention by not allowing him free rein in his experimentation. And so it could be deduced with an emotional illogic that they were directly responsible for the latest calamity as well.

"What is it all worth?" he asked now that the whole universe was arrayed against him and harrying him so closely. In that moment, even Venus, of whom it is known was once a proud and brave though foolish soldier of combat engineers, a non-commissioned officer among the sappers entrusted with one of the most difficult jobs in this galaxy—the firm erection of a sustainable Dome for the preservation of a species—in that moment of despair he too was tempted to abandon his life to the whirlpools of the Enemy and call in those servants whose function it is to annihilate the qualities that describe sentient existence.

The emotional character armor that had kept his face turgid and angry for decades hung heavy on him; and he felt that his face was suspended almost before him, ghostly and more heavy than uranium, while the rest of him, hopeless and vulnerable, suffered like a pink worm behind it. Horrified, Venus swung his head away and staggered a few steps from the tower. He felt like he might collapse but he didn't. A mouthless scream permeated the air and everything around him as his fingers clawed the air.

Burning with anguish he turned about gazing disgustedly at all his towers. Their ominous coolness projected like a horde of fangs in some gruesome primeval fishmouth below the abyss. The fairest young girls and young women any male eye could ever hope to behold were leaning this way and that from the narrow windows of the needle-like obelisks like so many flowers twisting in the sunlit breeze, trying to get a view of their master and mate. Their voices called down to him like little birds. But he ignored them now in his hollow heart. Empty memories, almost disappeared, how in the most romantic prince's garb he had seduced them each one at various stages of their lives with the wild delicacy and fanatic firmness that virgin girls swoon over. Having no one else like him to compare him with, they began by believing in everything he said and did. Many of them were now in the last stages of pregnancy. Their minds were just as swollen with hope. They all looked the same to him.

The towers spun around him a dozen times and Venus collapsed on the brittle lava floor. His mind struggled futilely to reproduce a new plan from the ashes of this one. He stabbed at possible directions the obsession of his heart might've taken. Not once could he formulate a lucid reason for her behavior, which he took for horrible ungratefulness. Insane, perhaps. For Venus had been an extremely loyal lover in his own way, and in fact there were many lesser females still going about their inglorious lives in the poverteous outskirts of the Dome that would have considered Venus's tower not such a difficult task, if only they could have shown themselves in their pretty clothes to the folks back home once or twice. Venus could not believe it--and he was going to give her the world, the whole world! All of his struggles—what was it all worth? Now she had gone, betrayed him in a flight that was tantamount to allegiance with those who had tried to keep him down every step of the way. Between terrible and pitiful longings Venus considered one thousand variations of revenge against her one thousand-fold. The two halves of his powerful mind like two sides of an ancient coin inimical to each other; like a body rejecting a transplanted organ at war with itself; it exhausted him, and Venus fell asleep, something he hadn't done for decades.

[Major Bunder here, because this is a good place to pause within this TransmuCast from a lost though duly decorated Scout. I will play the chorus, if you so please, your Excellency. Our emotion, whatever chemical apparatus has been provoked in our respective systems, must settle.

I am gazing solemnly upon my memory of the foregoing. The first character wishes in terror to enter a cage. The second is fleeing from every resemblance of one. And the third lusts to imprison another. It seems to me that there should be a fourth, your Excellency that longs to set another free. That would be a ginger group. But in point of fact there was no such spontaneous emergence on planet Earth in the era referred to here, as we now know; the population was devoid of her liberties. That being said, there were certainly enough charlatans within the reflecting Dome. Enough to channel the sluggish *sentiments of the human race into the usual domestic upgrades. That's what family duty does for you, if I may be so bold as to make a little joke, your Excellency. But still, some of their demagogues weren't all wrong, were they? By now they couldn't afford to be. For example, the Faction in the Dome's Council (re est circa 2nd DE 256) that later became so powerful by suggesting a careful exodus out of the Dome—they were not fools, and neither was their leader. The species owes not a small bit to him. The Jewelry Faction was baroque, but cunning enough indeed in matters of peace and war, and I daresay we'll hear more of them later in this very TransmuCast.*

Your Excellency, as you know, our Rangers' activities were blocked by an obstacle on this planet. You know our objective. In a case like this, only someone within that halted existence can evoke some inner change by becoming the fourth character I imagined.]

I

Despite his clutching fingers Acel was dragged out of the cell across the hard cold ground. The sun had set, red, invisible behind a red clouded sky.

'I want to stay in the cage! Wait!' he cried desperately but was ignored.

Acel was pulled into a large white longhouse and hurled onto a thickly rug-strewn floor. The door was shut behind him and fastened. Inside it was pitch black.

The air was warm and he began to sweat. The breath of others could be heard and felt. They seemed to be standing in a circle around him. Acel's heart beat in his ears. Some strange sense of recollection struck him and he gaped about.

A light under transparent plastic was lit behind them, shadowing their faces. Men, old, straight, some not so straight. One of them spoke, an old man's voice, in a ponderous singsong accent with an edge like fire and blizzards.

'The Cube has compelled us to break our procreant custom regarding this stud. We have always obeyed the dictates of the Cube, since they have preserved us through war and desolation. My heart tells me we should continue to do so. For long years the Cube has been silent, silent. And now its silence has been mysteriously lifted with news about this vessel. We all felt it, we all agree on the message. My head, old as it is, does not comprehend the reason in these new commands. Reflect with me.'

'Are you asking whether we should obey this new command?' a sour voiced elder queried.

'The Cube has never betrayed us! The Cube is the backbone of our society! What are you afraid of?' others challenged.

'I do not question,' another old voice, milder and firm, spoke from across the council's leader. 'When we lived in the dry grass, the heartshaped continent still slowly turning on a hotpink sea long times after the implosion of the universe of our fathers' fathers, then our herds were numerous. Mine alone numbered three thousand head, and I was not reckoned a wealthy man. But richly we ate. Sons we bore. And when the unspeakable reptilian hordes came over the world the Cube under the Man-shaped Boulder spoke to our prince. "Your grandfather, known to the universe as a Renegade since TransmuDream, father of your nation which has survived two universal catastrophes, planted this Cube here to instruct you," it said. "Dig me up," it said. "Let the clans of your men carry me north according to the compass, in a group of 36 and then 12 and then 42 and then 30, without deviation. Reach the Land Bridge that will raised again for you, as it was in the oldest days. Let one man leave this sum before you turn west and follow with groups of 20 and 15 and 61. Allow no man to touch the gelatinous substance of my heart within, no matter how it may slosh and splish around, or he will surely die insane! Take me to the cold hills yonder when the expanse of your land turns once more with the third moon, and cross over to the larger continent."—and we did so, with our herds. Bryn Las alone wished us to linger and lead our herds through that northern plain to feed, against the urging of prince Seajohn to whom the message came before it came to all. That plain, we found, was not clean. We lost many head there, and we lost our seed too. I was a tiny boy when the cells of Bryn Las's body were decimated and given to the females to trample, unfit for fodder! Our pitiable prince, his line's blood in him still pretty hot, destroyed himself that night in disgust at his body's loss and also because Bryn Las was his half brother. Still, we evaded the unspeakable horde. And a message came to all the elders of the blood. The Cube showed us new high planes with sparse grass but enough for our present existence. And we took out dwelling here on Snow Mountain. The Cube dictated the nature of our raiders then, to take studs from the Outskirts of the hideous Great Dome which our people have never run with (we love the open spaces). The Cube taught us how to use them, without lending fever to our females. I have thought a long time about this. The Cube has never shown us how to get back our seed, nor promised to do so. You are the eldest of the line, Gord SeaRon. Could this be a sign toward that secret hope which even we cannot suppress?'

'Idiot number one.'

'No self control whatsoever!'

'Nature's machinery at its finest.'

'A fool is a special thing.'

'Very special!'

'There's nothing wrong with me and the way things are right now!'

Acel listened in wonder at these speeches. It was like something out of one of his old books, a better one, but happening in front of him. The arcane diaspora of these people across a psychically shaped continent, a Cube full of secrets like the things insane Venus raved on about—and now revolving around himself!

'Don't think about the females!' the leader, Gord SeaRon shouted at them all to quiet them down. 'They get old so quickly, but they die so slowly.'

But this only enflamed a new spout of arguing among these elders—amidst harsh laughter. That mysterious Cube, their women, this incredible history, all these subjects hurled at each other maliciously—in a throbbing background of their horrible sterility.

Acel didn't think he could stand it. Was his destiny, the end of his life, to be meted out in this cacophony of eunuchs? He determined that he wasn't going to die without a fight and he could fight all these old men, he could take them out, break their knees, take one hostage ...

A face came near him. He could almost make out the long warm beard, wide face. Who spoke so long about themselves. Warmth exuded from this person.

'You might as well just go through with it, boy. Right through that curtain over there. These icicles will never give up what little they have. Go ahead. Get up and walk past me, keep going, you'll reach it.'

Acel could see no curtain in this dark but he didn't want to stay here. He got up as silently as he could and circled around behind the arguing old men. He drew his hands along the wall which was covered in some kind of heavy cloth and plastic. He moved quickly, his pulse beating with the wildest urge to escape before anyone else noticed.

Finally his fingers found a space between the sheets, warmer than the room. He turned sideways and pushed through. The sheets and tarps hung with cold dense weight over his shoulders and body, reminding him of his weakness and his mortality. The air became humid, frightening. He was entering another dream, from a nightmare.

Suddenly Acel burst into a marvelous room. He was shouting, 'I am 33 years old! I love life!' And then he was through. His eyes riveted on the most amazing thing he had ever seen. It was not a TransmuCast, but Acel was slipping into the trancelike dream he feared. With effort he kept aloof, struggling for his mind, watching this thing in front of him.

It was perched on an altar carved with intricate designs, of the Outlanders' oppressive imagination. A light of shimmering blue issued from it illuminating the floor up to where Acel stood. A cube, a meter across in every dimension, of the clearest and strongest crystal—it must have been the same sacred material from which the Dome itself was constructed! It looked like an aquarium without fish, without sand or shells. But the marvelous liquid contained within swirled and swished with a life of its own. It was completely entrancing.

Acel raised his hand to shield his eyes from such a meaningful and fascinating sight, driving his mind down to concentrate on his body, on his location, other surroundings. But lining the walls were further delights to him: shelves and shelves of books! Old books, Acel could tell, real books with good subjects that he could get his teeth into, his brains into, historical subjects, the secrets of humanity at last!

Breaking from the spell of the Gelatinous Cube, Acel leapt toward the nearest stack and gingerly pulled the first volume from its shelfmates. It was large and yellow, bound in old pressed leather. Tears of sweetness came to his eyes in the humid silence. With both hands he lifted it up inhaling the woody musty scent of its pale paper, and spread it open somewhere in the middle.

Few words danced across the bottom of the pages revealed. Strange looking words in a language he did not understand. The characters were legible but perhaps he did not yet know these words. He looked quickly up to the picture they seemingly described. It was a drawing of rolling fields of war. In fact it was hideous and war seemed too small a word to describe the scene presented. It began in the rolling fields of a fertile countryside, which Acel had never seen. But now he could smell the black earth moist and tilled, upturned and recently sown with the loving fingers of its farmers, who knew how to coax life and nourishment from the ancient soil. An empty white sky hung overhead, filling the attention with scenes closer in. Fences built to contain livestock could not keep out the invading horde. The work was trampled by such an army as made Acel disbelieve his eyes. A feeling of mysterious evil enshrouded him. Reptilian demonoids cackling and champing their jaws, foul tongues dangling and flicking, weaving tails and waving tridents, nets and various ugly forward-curving blades they poured forth myriad, bunching at the places where human species seemingly had its last stand. There where the rails of the last fence broke down, a scattered remnant of soldiers, militia, and menfolk attempted to hold off this massacre with whatever household tools came to hand. Behind them could be seen clearly their homes and rough houses, women bundling away the screaming children with a last forlorn glance at their only hope as they fled the inevitable.

Acel did not know what it meant, or when this picture, which seemed so true to life, was from. But within the book and near its place on the shelf he only found more of the same terrible subject. Others were covered in elegant geometric charts with alienlike scripts he couldn't make heads or tails of. There were maps of underground cities sprawled beneath barren desert. Hieroglyphs, computations, gigantic men with six fingers and six toes, donning horsehead helmets, carrying away beautiful women from flaming cities. Many of the images were engraved on rolled strips of stinking pale leather, which made the eeriness much worse.

Acel quickly stepped away on to another area of the library. But as he was in the act of doing so, it suddenly occurred to him that he had heard that madman Venus mention such a struggle with those lizard armies and human life. He could not be sure. All of this was a depiction of the Secret History he craved but could not fathom.

So many books he'd never seen! Never imagined!

He was across the room. By now his body felt in every inch the insufferable weight of an eye upon him. It was gaining again, the visions. The weight was of exactly a million flowers on his head. An attention was bathing his back fiercely just like the terrible Hot Season under the Dome; his every simple gesture harshly scrutinized, a caustic laser searing the world. It was coming from the Cube, but he didn't dare to turn and look at it again.

Like a plant he lifted another volume from its shelf, he was so sluggish and tediously pathetic. These are the moments which carve a man's character. This one was older than the first but not as old as the scrolls. Dust was launched from its surface making Acel sneeze twice in tears—which became terror ... but no, he could not hear the old counselors; he was left alone ... alone with the Living Cube breathing down his back.

Acel flipped open the book rather too cavalierly. Long paragraphs met him and he bravely began one. The sentences were difficult to follow for Acel because they were so long and complex, like drawing a stretch of black silk before his eyes and comprehensively following every distinct glitter in a stream of diamonds; it painted a picture of a young man in an agony of livid conscience. In its long lapping wave Acel found it difficult not to believe that he was this young man on the run, in a mental way, from his Dome's Homeguard, and that he was doing something at this moment despicable to all the individual mores of his species. And for all that Acel found himself physically restraining his own hilarity. The personalities introduced were very endearing to him and it was beautiful. Acel took a deep breath, sighed slightly, and closed the cover of this relic. He put the book back in its place so carefully, intentionally without looking at it. For some reason he thought of pitiful Church outside in his cage, insane. Such books could help people. He'd never known that men could write such revealing things, beautiful things.

With strength of will Acel tried another book. He was relieved to find short sentences arranged in a column. But so many words were unfamiliar to him. And there were no pictures. He could eventually construct a meaning at sentence level though in the multifarious collision of vocabulary. But very strangely, again it seemed the story of a young man, and this one couldn't make up his mind because he also was in the madcap throes of numerous consciences. It was crazy, in fact Acel found himself raving with laughter at the dialogue between anyone there. Why, are all these books about the emotions in a mind, Acel asked. The words were crazy too. Acel thought of his youth up to now, was he crazy? Outside was the snow, and how far was it back home?

Acel's own words could not fully express the richness of the treasure he felt he'd discovered. If only the people he knew in the Dome could read and understand books like this one, like all of these! He might find a friend ... after so many increasingly isolated years in the Dome ... That he might find a friend. Well, well, what a well.

Now Acel turned to face the power that had dogged and attracted him. The whispering golden gelatinous water. Whispering his name like golden bells of light.

His hands and face were bathed in the exhilarating glow of warmth. He stood over it exulting. Below his outstretched fingers the liquid shimmered. Acel felt like he could build a universe with it. This was that primal material, he thought.

Suddenly without premeditation he plunged his hands into the Gelatinous Cube. Lightning struck his mind. He did not have to build universes, they were already built, sprawling out before him with intricate designs in more directions than conceivable. Like immense colorful sea creatures they were each drifting rolling inexorably to the center of his consciousness, an intimacy he could not imagine, fearing to, where it would surely be unbearable sensation—then

Multiverse was pouring through him. Without Time or Space the man watched his body die, grow, and be born in increasingly rapid succession. Flowers covered the laughing liquid of the Cube. A chorus of ecstatic blue voices of children welcomed him. The song caressed him to the very marrows, spun honey from his marrow and drew it out like electric taffy, the little precious tongues of the angels playing his body like the strings of a chemical harp. Acel remained, swaying, and could not feel alone again, he could not struggle.

Another voice began to swell from the cracked subjectivity of his experience. Every word blazed at him with complete definition, and yet it seemed some time before he could make sense of what was being said.

' ... At last it's you. It is really you. I have been calling you all your life, as I was assigned to do, beckoning to you more strongly since you left the sheltering Dome.'

Someone has been calling me with their mind, Acel's thought fired in response. The visions, those terrible clairvoyant plunges outside the Dome. Someone touching me through this Cube. All the Cubes. This subconscious transmitter on my planet. The lowest level pulse. I had dreams. I've had a feeling since I was born, a feeling of purpose. It was a thirst that drank deeply whenever I left the Dome and stood in the sand near the old vineyards. My mind gave way in clairvoyant visions as we drew nearer this moment.

'Circumstances have prevailed. Common with your species.'

Acel's brain filled with whispers that made strange sense. All that we've planned ... I remember my name ... remember my name ... all that we've planned ... the heart of the Cosmos ...

'Who are you?' Acel asked suddenly.

'I am He-Whose-Name-You-Do-Not-Know. I am not your Enemy. Do you know who *you* are?'

And there were lives, as if from a thousand dreams, all come back to Acel. Among them, over them, there was one consistent string of events that magnetized his mind; again and again his thought stumbled over an image of himself in mid-gesture in some alien situation—only to find himself grasping at nothing, at air, it slipped by as he was in mid-gesture looking down through another image of himself. Again and again, like a serpent showing its greasy scales through the water, first here, then there, like something was showing through the fluid visage of life. Acel was inconceivably attracted to it, desperately. It was always just behind the next welcoming wave of liquid gelatinous angelic fluid. A torture, an identity-spark he was losing his mind pursuing—

'Do I know?'

Acel reeled but his hands were locked in the living water of the Cube. All of this happened in a delirious second but suddenly the voice was asking something else, hard to determine, something so very important.

'Have you found the obstacle?'

'Obstacle?'

The voice struck him like the crack of a whip.

'Don't you remember?'

And suddenly he did remember. It was thrust into his brain. The words were his own, but they were not from his own mouth, not from his same life, and yet there was some quality by which he remembered them as eternally his own. Even his lips moved with them.

There is an obstacle to my Device, some force of resistance on the planet which hitherto was not present.

Where was this conversation? Acel was remembering himself from another perspective.

There is an obstacle to my Device, some force of resistance on the planet which hitherto was not present.

Now the figure of Sir Venus soared to Acel. This man, with all his vanities and crimes, terrible crimes and terrible vanities. His bizarre machine he bragged of, that he invented to usurp the power of the authorities who had outcast him. That was the obstacle which perverted contact and prevented the angels from manifesting their will on Earth.

'Yes, I have found the obstacle,' he answered at last.

'Then you must remove it.'

At these sharp instructions a sudden rage swelled up in Acel. He could not say why. The directive of his mission was clear, the insistence of a truer life, a purpose in life—a truth for which people would have sold their souls in the anemic Dome, if it was only possible. He must destroy the obstacle that prevented assistance and nourishment of his species. He was human. He had always been of these people, this world.

But that was just it, wasn't it? Venus, for all of the inhuman things he had done, was still very human indeed. Acel could see that now; it was written in every gesture the suffering and outrageous man made, in a million strokes of conceit and passionate ambition. He may have originated in an earlier era, as seemed likely, and more properly be called a correlation of human elements, or an awful archaic ruin, but he still belonged to humanity somehow after all; he belonged to Acel and Acel must claim him. There was no way he would betray even the most monstrous criminal to an inhuman judgement. Despite the loyalty of a previous life in a shattered age, of even the most benevolent organization in the Cosmos ... Venus's fate must be left to human laws. The idea of intrusion by others was as odious as the puerile workings of the Enemy which led to Venus's excesses.

'The obstacle has been identified,' he swallowed. 'It is the result of human invention. Misguided urges. Abundant urges ... To better a depleted condition,' he added sadly.

'Well, you see to it, Captain Rice.' The presence commanded, its last words laden with the kind of sarcasm that incites poor humans to remember their duty. He-Whose-Name-We-Do-Not-Know was aware of the enormous disturbance, vaguely rebellious, that emanated up from Acel across the planes, though he didn't understand the sense of it. Nevermind, he concluded, so long as the organism is pushed into extraordinary deeds by an altruism it can hardly process. Captain Rice will be no more after the success of Deeply Privileged.

'Perform your duty well. Your species is counting on you ... Re-enter and assist. Re-enter and assist ...'

Earthly coordinates were given Acel as to where the Outlanders had originally dug up the present Cube. He was warned to commit them to memory, and never to reveal them to another human as long as he lived. He has not and they are hidden in this work.

Acel was once more left bathing in the warm living water. Solitary and yet not alone, with uncounted tongues of honey revealing the vastness of a Multiverse in shifting sensual refractions. Acel drowsed in pleasure.

Within his mind he composed the memories which formed almost all of this book so far as you have read it. They were transmitted through the Cube almost before he realized it. And they were deployed as he considered them, through a mind floating in the rich memory of a Gelatinous Cube, a pretty insecure medium.

Excerpts of another conversation dripped through his thoughts then, from before he was born, words from mouths with vorpal faces trembling behind Councils swathed in secretude and darkness.

'Their Dome's days are numbered. It will not survive even you.'

'Who doesn't know that?

'Our directive and my orders are to re-enter and assist. I will find the cause of the obstacle to our investigation. They will not be destroyed by a love which ... which ...'

'The years are numbered, Rice. Remove the obstacle and your species may survive.'

Who was she? There was someone else. He had not entered alone. No, they were supposed to enter together, born as human twins, to assist each other. To re-enter and assist. They were not born as twins, not even in the same family. Something awful stirred in Acel. Where were her reports? She had made none. These were only the remembrances of what they had said to each other before the greatest adventure conceivable to either of them. Where was she now? Krystal, beautiful lovely Krystal, where was she now?

'The Enemy is always pressing us, Rice. Many are those who perish between worlds. I know of no report from them.'

Oh, but Krystal, we were coming to be born and to live and to die in confidence. How was it our hands became separated during the majestic stasis ascending, hurtling, the horizontal fall ...? Was our Device so weak? No, no, my dearest Krystal. But I checked every gelatinous joint, every infinitesimal bolt of the quantum machinery—

Acel's soul heated and turned in agonizing turmoil, his mind dancing with a memory he could not accept. Just before dissolution, had she really done that, had she really opened her hand and ... just let go?

That was not her training. They had both been briefed, instructed with all possible care toward memory retention. Krystal Elioud had abandoned Deeply Privileged and now she was on the opposite side of the world doing what no one understood.

Acel's brain worked and plodded itself into a supplemental report. He took care of its delivery. His mind,. with unanswered but expressed questions, rested.

Milliseconds or years could have passed before Acel drew his hands from the ever-unsated Cube. He found that he had urinated down his pantlegs; it was cold. On an inspiration he took them off and rinsed the groin areas clumsily through the gelatinous waters of the wondrous Cube. This was a tremendous experience that in summary once again reminded Acel that there was a very important job to do. His was this mission and he wondered at it and loved it, especially when he considered the fantastic technology which facilitated his own birth here; in a world he had always known and taken for granted, especially when he noticed it dissatisfying him. And this dreamlike reality that now gave him a purpose such as he'd longed for too long to remember how long, there was nothing he wouldn't do for it. If he could find Venus's ridiculous but cunningly glorious invention, he must destroy it. And yet ... was this mandate all there was to his life?

The young man could not imagine what his destiny would be after that. But he hoped he would be allowed just to go home, and see his mom again at last.

II

Acel strode out into the snow with his pants in his hand. He was amused to see the Outsiders of the cold mountains all sitting spread out in front of him waiting for his appearance. He noticed how thin they all were, rugged and thin. The morning light lit their expectant faces like streaming colored glass. Automatically he stopped in front of the elders where they sat. 'The Doctor, Doctor,' they murmured several times. 'He is drenched in the Living Water!'

A hush went over the crowd.

Five young men stood and came to him carrying long willowy spears. They kept their faces down. They had bundles and packs, ready for a long journey. At this point Acel put his pants back on. He didn't have anything to say to these people.

He strode across the cold ground toward Church's cage. The Outsiders edged aside quickly and the scout-like youths followed behind him. Acel felt mildly confident; they would not touch him, they couldn't even dare to do so now. That Cube was all they knew. Minding his posture Acel approached the ridiculous little cage.

'Church! Get up! I'm unlocking this gate here for you, you're set free! After a thousand nights, I bet!'

Church rolled toward him like a worm and peered from his blankets.

'It's been long enough! Come out!' Acel called over feeling pretty jocular. In a huge crescent around them crept the silent Outlanders, speechlessly. His young escort milled around behind him staring at their feet obviously embarrassed.

Church's head craned out. His mouth was a straight line across the bottom of his face, his moustache above it. This expression set Acel to laughing hard, but Church kept looking out so timidly and yet so unbelievingly that Acel laughed even harder.

Finally Church spoke.

'Maybe they have screwed the daylights out of you, boy, you're glowing like a business cone. But I'm not going out to do the same and I've made myself clear since the beginning of all this.'

'Since the—since the—bikini?' Acel could not control himself. Even the young men behind had begun to chuckle shyly.

'The beginning! The beginning of all this madness, this world of denial and temptation, *my* world, you poor intoxicated foolish mortal dust devil! I've seen so many of you go, so many of you go that way. Did I think you were different? Maybe I did. Especially when you got dragged out like that. But all the guys go down the same fatal silken path once they're out of this cage, so I don't go out, do I? No. Not if you bring the whole populace out here, Acel. That was a nice thing to do, maybe a nice touch. But you can forget it.'

With an easy gesture Acel pulled the little gate open and held it in his hand, surprised that it didn't exhibit any sturdier resistance. A child could come out of this trap, he thought. I sure didn't realize that.

This alarmed Church.

'You're doing everything the extraordinary way,' he said.

'Come out of there, Church. You're wasting my time as much as you ever have. We're not going into the sex shack now. We're going to the Dome. Or we should go near enough there so that you can go back in. These people won't stop us now.'

Acel glanced back over the crowd who all lowered their heads in respect and fervent hope. The Doctor? he thought. I'm not so sure about that, but it makes sense to play it off until we get through.

'I have been commissioned by the Gelatinous Cube to bring back the cure to your sterility. It won't be long now! I have touched our most secret sacred water and I live right in front of you!' Acel shouted over the crowd.

The people were astonished and jubilantly cowered backwards.

Church was no moron and he squirmed out of the cage in a second. His expression was still nervous as he considered Acel's appearance and his words.

'Let's start immediately then, um, what about nourishment?' he asked.

'If I'm not mistaken, Church, those five young men are accompanying us. I don't know how far ...'

'Yes, I've seen them before.'

The young men displayed their bags slightly and stepped forward. Their leader possessed an ironic curve of smile.

'My name is Yana. We are strong and trustworthy, you'll see. We'll accompany you as far as the cure, and back when you require it. We'll guard you and our interests.'

'I'm sure you will,' Church muttered.

As if in response their new strange scouts brought out dried meat for the two Dome-men who took some handfuls and began chewing. They also handed tinted mirror-like spectacles to the men which they put on. Church obviously enjoyed them. With that began their long journey toward west.

'This is the way,' Acel told Church's questioning look. 'I'm sure of it.'

'You're a changed man, Acel. I don't know how, but you're a changed man.'

III

The intelligence being reported back to the Council of Captain Rice's discovery by one of the Cubes was heartening to everyone involved with planet Earth. It was a matter of simple geometry, cubing the sphere, to disclose to him the placement of the others if he needed it. He would merely have to plot where the Outlander humans had found their Cube before bringing it to their new cold lands. The intelligence had been given to him, if only he would use it and never lose it. This could be nothing more than a positive step in the right direction. It was also a reward for deeply feeling He-Whose-Name-We-Do-Not-Know, who had made Rice's recovery into a kind of personal vendetta against the ubiquitous powers of the Enemy. Since his first contact with the Outlanders he had remained constantly transmitting a surge of his directed mind into the obstacle'd obscurity of our striving planet, hoping to finger out our brave and unknown scout and pull him in to the necessary, if shocking, briefing.

Though they could not see all of it, the world glimpsed by the Council through Rice's eyes caused some sigh of relief. This was evident from the tone of a long memo circulated by Major Arthur Bunder afterward, which Rice later accessed with many of the archives that interested him. The situation was developing exactly as expected, from what had been observed last just before the strange eclipse that brought on Deeply Privileged. Namely, the resources of the Dome being finally exhausted at the pre-coordinated time in which much of the Earth's bizarre radio-activity was becoming dissipated enough that life could flourish again, a migration must begin outward. Back into the unknown world. The gamble of Earth's second Dome was poised to be won or lost.

There were new flora and fauna to classify (and devour), waters to discover, new geologies to take account of, new continents to explore and map, a new mortal empire to build. The total population of the Dome at this time was around 400 million souls incapacitated with the painkilling TransmuCast. It would take an enormous effort to galvanize them into their new duty for life, and that is why observation and close-presence monitoring were assumed to be so important by those concerned with the history of our species. But this had been unaccountably blocked. So Deeply Privileged was given the go-ahead by Major Bunder (and his esteemed superiors) once Rice had volunteered for it.

No Cosmic Rangers operation is run according to complete omniscience, and usually if something can go wrong it does go wrong. This can often be explained in terms of putrid Enemy action. And something did go wrong—where was Krystal Elioud? However in this case something also went right. By the time Captain Rice really recovered his mission born into the world as Acel Daniel and had identified the obstacle he was sent to neutralize, an unlooked-for development was going according to plan with our surprisingly sturdy human race. To comprehend it one must take a cursory look at what passed for politics in the transparent Dome.

Scenario review: The Dome was governed by a technocracy that was also a plutocracy. The controllers of the TransmuCast lived in relative splendor on its constant tax paid to them by the citizens of the Dome and had no interest in relinquishing even a tiny share of their own dwindling resources. That's what had become of the heirs of TransmuDream's vestigial Device: penny-counting electronic pharmacists assisting a Domed nation into doomed slumber. One day the denizens of the Earth's Dome would awaken outraged to a power outage, and that's just what happened, while their leaders, who met only in fantastic nearly solipsist Councils, were still languishing in an indulgent resource which was their privilege.

Riot tore the Business Zones apart and emptied the market halls, the program accountants' pointed towers. Crowds fleeing pell-mell, the obese bodies with little pointed heads. Some of them had just arrived, laboriously mounting the steps when their own kind rushed back out at them, trampling them in terror below the Domed shadow of a Business Cone. Brilliant in the Dome's heat they were abandoned with shattered glass, lost shoes, wires and plastic scraps—like a gigantic puppet had exploded on impact dropped from somewhere higher than the Dome. The killing and destroying instinct, the great pleasure in destruction, still a strong contender. Human rage always poised to pour out. Always willing to get its fear organized into machineries of cruelty and annihilation. Finding one lust impossible, we leap into another with claws extended and tongue hanging. This was a reaction no one would have expected from such a people. But the causes are not now invisible to you, though the plot was amateurish compared to a Cosmic Ranger's constant Multiversal diplomacy. Awakening from an illogical stupor, the Supermarket on the same morning reported a lack of reserves. The Homeguard, which was not trained to handle a total disruption of the society to which they and their families belonged, collapsed into hunting fragments and individuals armed inside their fortified homes. Anarchy's terrible sword was unsheaved and humanity's back was to the glassine wall.

If, on the morning that Acel Daniel set out from the Outlanders' snowy highlands, he could've seen the inordinate amount of hideously colored smoke pouring from the exhaust ventilation system of the Dome, his distant home, he would've been seized with distress and trepidation for his family. Luckily for him now he was very far away. No, on the scene in the chaos instead the man of the day was General Frankfurt of the Homeguard, a esteemed member of the populist Jewelry Faction. This faction had been so named because of his family's enormous contribution to advertising on TransmuCast. Of course there was only one brand of anything and this did not make their job easier. Their niche was they handled everything to do with creature vanity among an obesifying populace. Something that most people familiarized themselves with was a dreamy sequence in celebration of a synthetic sympathetic ruby, in which the viewers continually felt they were being pulled inside its delicious core (hence the name ascribed to Frankfurt's faction). This episode became extremely popular before the crises, and a swelling majority of Dome citizens tuned into it again and again. Soon everyone was sporting the Frankfurt family's jewels.

Frankfurt himself was no mean customer. And not only in his prescience to invest in a stock of desperate sexually aggressive messages in his advertisements, which later led to the absolutely surprising margin of gross violence from a desperate, spoiled and starving population. And not only in his habitually luscious apparel either. He was a powerful man with a thick neck, balding head and a massively hawkish nose. He leaned his head forward when he spoke with someone, peering at them from under his yellow brows with a slow even fixation that seemed to want to singe the air. But most of the time he did not concentrate his powers on any individual this way. It was enough to stride around with his huge chest thrust out malevolently shouting, "Splendid indeed!" while his staff scattered about doing the bidding of his blue and chipped index fingers which long service or immediate terror ennured them to interpret. Except for the slightest proturbation of a gut, Frankfurt was a portrait of mature commanding vitality and masculine health.

Like all the Dome nabobs and scions who made up the ruling Council of the Wise, dynamic Frankfurt knew not only that their energy and resources were running out, but when. He was a master at debt analysis. Frankfurt was different in that he had prepared for it, he had a plan, he had vision. None of this did he share with the fellows of his social sphere who seemed to be paralyzed in opulence, unable to consider squarely the consequences of nature before they rolled over in despair and exhaustion and plunged once more into the oblivion of the

TransmuCast. For them this held a special narcissistic flavor since most of them were responsible for some organic portion of its current programs' designs. It was an inescapable fruit of delight for them to become another, for instance, inside a wondrous dream that they had created, and to emerge again at just the right second as themselves. Frankfurt thought these lazy self-indulgent nabobs no better than the common mass whom long tradition had appointed them to lead.

Although Frankfurt was as surprised, or rather as shocked as everyone else by the sudden chaos and violence of Area 1, etc, his own long-laid plans were awaiting his command. He was no fool nor was he lazy, and he comprehended the cyclical market of necessary commodities. Frankfurt had already filled warehouses with supplies against the day he had seen coming, when human explorers would temeritously creep out of a deadening Dome looking for more life and sustenance for life. And he would own the monopoly with the only new initial public offerings. If else anyone had cared or dared to ponder this inevitability, they might've done the same. But predictably enough, they hadn't, at least not effectively; maybe no one who had considered it could afford to. Frankfurt knew when to buy when panic was imminent. The other members of the Council of the Wise were more inclined to invite their minds to grope around for some impossible method of sustaining or budgeting what they already had and were steadily losing. Selling was rampant. Only Frankfurt had the vision to plan instead for the day we must increase our food, our lands, our nourishment—or totally die out in a real ugly scene not on TransmuCast. The swift implosion of the Business Cones' population and the burning barbaric strife that followed in the Zone of the Area only meant that he would either have to adjust the prices he'd planned for his stock with the demand and danger of the mob. As the situation spread by the second, Frankfurt stayed on top of his investment with a whole network of runners and messengers.

Of course not the entire Dome was in rebellion. There were meeker Areas who formed androidlike queues and waited futilely for rations; who stared dumbly at their blank screens and dead hardware and appliances and finally at each other waiting for something to talk about; who hid frightened waiting and began to slowly perish in unknown places. They were too subdued by a lifelong diet of playing TransmuCast to do anything else. Frankfurt's method was he forgot about them.

Therefore, using the skeleton battalions of the Homeguard still left to him, Frankfurt was able to centralize a semblance of rule in many of the Areas adjacent to his own and to the most chaotic Zone. Because order was already disturbed there he found it easier to impose a new one. Areas 1 though 11 and 13 were fortified and reorganized with objectives along a logistic route of scout and supply. Always optimistic, Frankfurt figured that within one year he could have 47% of the Dome population living in communal farms outside the Dome, which he supplied, even if he had to do it at gunpoint in some cases. Splendid indeed. To the devil with the rest.

IV

They had been walking far when Church, trying to grow used to his new freedom, began conversation with Acel. He asked him in a low voice what had happened when "those numbnut Outlanders" took him away.

Acel tried to explain about the Cube of warm living water. He knew there were eight of them placed evenly around the world—cubing the sphere—once one was discovered the others could be found easily. To leave his hands in the water absorbing indefinitely, to ingest the beauteous liquid … the future of all possibilities. That was the path toward TransmuDream, toward the godlike abilities … perhaps toward the Cosmic Rangers. His mind brimmed in secret with the coordinates given him and he'd written them on scraps of paper with a pen he always carried.

'That sounds like something from the Cosmic Rangers!' Church said.

'It's a technology very advanced. But the Outlanders aren't responsible for it. It came about before the TransmuDream Implosion …'

'Before the Dome?'

'Yes, before the world as we know it, Church. At some point what was called nano technology—microscopic machinery on the molecular level—used primarily for medical purposes until it was unfortunately used as weaponry—at some point it was translated to a liquid medium. At that time there already existed atomic maps of various brains deemed important to our species. It was the next step to program one into a container of this liquid using the molecular technology. The result was an active mind that began at that brain's map. Though without a body of instincts to care for, it became mystic! A mind aware of itself as part of everything, pure awareness … After some experimentation a certain communicability was noticed. Like a transistor. But a verifiable interface was never really realized between our scientists and the saint they had created. Even though each of their lives was profoundly affected by contact with it. Eventually the current government found its own uses. In a curious information leak this Cube became the prime ingredient to the TransmuDream technology that threatened our universe and all but destroyed the civilizations of our planet .'

'You seem to know a lot about it!'

'I've read about these things all my life. I had to find the books myself …'

This was half true, because what Acel was now repeating was only partly construed from what he remembered reading. In fact he was surprised at his own articulation.

Church muttered, 'Books, huh?' and was silent for a while. There was only the crunching of their boots in the snow.

'You said there were eight of those Cubes—'

'Cubes.'

'That's what I said. So you said there were eight of them. Were they all filled with brains? And whose brains were used anyway?'

'Only one. The first one. One was enough. It was a scientist named Einstein. At one time he was supposed to be quite an eminent human being. Revolutionized science …'

'Well I don't know about science, Acel, but maybe I've got my own theories. Theories that just cooked themselves in my brain while I was sitting in these numbnut bastards' cage all those months.'

'About marital constancy?' Acel's old wry grin showed through again.

'No … not exactly. Maybe…. What was it like before TransmuDream, Acel? As far as you have read, I mean, were men and women always married together and … expected to be? I figure maybe people are always the same, have always been the same. That's what my brain thinks in its cage. But I like to hear you talk, Acel. Stuff about those old times feels like some kind of anchor in this weird life.'

They passed some black scraggly trees. They were separated by one and had to go around. The silent Outlander snowmen were dark spots out front making jokes the two men could not hear or understand. They were happy to be going far out again; Acel knew they would go anywhere in the world for what they thought he could do for them. What could he do for them? That was only one of his worries and he'd rather not think about any of them yet.

'Yes, an anchor. Yes … You know, Church, that just before TransmuDream societies all over the world were changing themselves very abruptly.'

'What societies? More than one school, Homeguard …? Didn't the same government—?'

'No, the world was divided, they were nations, like all the Areas of the Dome scattered over the world without a common language. But communication technology brought it together in activity; large businesses influenced people. Imagine many Domes each with its own TransmuCast but buying and selling products and programs from each other—you understand the competition? In those days everyone had to pay someone else for land and housing, for the utility of harnessed nature such as piped water, like we do our TransmuCast, but everyone had to work more and more to do it. First all the men, then both sexes. Not like now—they'd work everyday, all day. They had to. One's own society was always expanding, trying to take over the others!'

'People seem the same to me so far.'

'Sure. Only now we're so lazy with self-indulgence we're just—'

'We're just waiting for time to run out.'

The two men glanced grimly into each others' protected eyes. Just as men of intelligence had done all over the Dome for the last score years.

'There's more too. They didn't stop there. These nations were competing for who could be richest and have the most and latest inventions. That kept people sharp and they got smarter too. Getting all the women to work same as the men, see, that doubled production, and it doubled the military. Soon all the nations wanted to do it. They were more powerful, people were buying luxuries, land, buying powers to buy more in a money market I'm still trying to understand. The thing is, this money system, its competition was rapacious! Mothers couldn't raise their children anymore now, they had to work. Families drifted apart, didn't see each other more than they had to. Educated children became independent entrepreneurs over the communication technology of the times. Kind of a limited TransmuCast called Web that just really changed their world and brought all the nations together in the market. The destruction of the family was pretty much complete I guess when TransmuDream got developed.'

'A sacrifice.' Church murmured. 'I wonder how much they are existing together now.'

Both men walked on, thinking of their families and of TransmuCast. Little did they know that the instigator of fantasy and boredom that had torn their families apart in various ways—Church to adultery, Acel to eccentricity of books and dissatisfaction—that the system adored and fed by all with all their time, the reality of the mortal empire of Earth's second Dome had already disintegrated.

So they walked many kilometers every day beneath a sky overcast and often thunderous. Sometimes it was trudging drudgery, cold misery. Others it was pleasant enough; it kept them warm. For both of them it was a constant wonder: nature, the world outside of the Dome. When the sun came up in the purple agony of dawn like pure sweet birth. When the sun filled the land with muted golden warmth lying like lace over the snow. The occasional bird winging haphazardly through the thin clinging cold. It was living, strange, vibrant, independent. And just a moment's comparison between the kind of outdoors adventure they were living now and humid grimy tedium of the Dome life they recalled caused furrows in their brows and made them think and talk.

Acel was very enthused having something he'd never felt before: a purposeful mission, a plan in his life. He walked like a new leader, almost like a Cosmic Ranger! Those Snowmen scouting ahead for him—even though he privately had no idea how their hopes would be fulfilled by him and their sterility cured. No, as delightful as all the new knowledge was for a Domeboy, its glimmer did tarnish somewhat, and Acel was not easy in his mind. In fact Acel's opinion had continued to resonate from a certain feeling he had had recently during his ecstatic and strange encounter in the Gelatinous Cube.

He kept thinking about Venus and his homemade Device that he was supposed to destroy. *Had been commanded to destroy.* Good intentions from another lifetime seemed to pale in certain ways. First, although it's true Venus was a terrible criminal by any social laws Acel had experience with, he was also not truly part of any society. He was a monster preying on its fringes. Or, Acel sometimes shuddered to think, was he the hero he believed himself to be? Impossible! Offensive to the concept. Repulsive even. And he is sweaty and his mouth smells. But Acel tried to look further … into a strange zone. Raw courage, yes. Indeed, Venus may have had the courage to stand up and say that man can decide for himself what is good for him. Or was this Acel's own imagination? Why did Venus bother to keep trying to broadcast his discoveries to those authorities he rejected? Why try? The means were already in his hands to fulfill his ambition, as Acel began to see it, since the Device was such an obstacle to the Rangers' Council. Why should vanity nullify what his marvelous pride helped create? They say they cannot assist humankind in the face of the Enemy with such an obstacle ... But was there a human advantage in that? ... Acel conceived that Venus just might have to be removed somehow after all, but increasingly he felt a swelling curiosity to have a close look at Venus's strange Device.

Or was this the very temptation of the Enemy?

Acel wanted to be wary of discussing too much with Church as they traveled together. He didn't care to trigger those pitiful landslides of emotion witnessed back in the cage. Church was a delicate audience who thought too much, like a prostrate patient absorbing the doctor's objective pronouncements. The Outlanders, anyway, still addressed Acel as Doctor. Besides all that, Acel was too busy remembering that other life, preoccupied with the larger world at large. Just as the reader of a poem connects a flow of events outside the page with these marching symbols, a key opening cryptic doors, wherever the encouraging author moves him.

Nonetheless, following the dictates of human nature, conversation often ensued beyond Church's frequent groping questions.

Shin-deep in crunching snow Church's brown eyes tightened behind his glasses and he'd ask something such as, 'What is the unique quality of the human soul?'

'What? As opposed to ...?'

'No, as opposed to himself. I mean, how is it developed from such a shattered background?'

Wishing to avoid Church's personal past, Acel answered, 'Consciousness—the more you have, the more spirituality you are capable of. That's the potential for development.'

'In which direction? Maybe I could take different views.' Church looked thoughtful and pained.

And Acel hurried to describe the unique qualities of faith, the focus and process of various fanatic old religions of Earth before TransmuDream that he used to enjoy so much reading about. The roots of humanity. 'If you consider all those unique and essential perspectives together, Mr Church, you will have a portrait of the human soul.'

By the time the nights came during this stage of their journey Acel began to tell him simply to refer to what he'd already told him during the time they'd known each other. He was too tired to repeat himself. Church was a monomaniac.

It was no exception when Church talked directly about his passion.

'I guess,' he'd ponder for long minutes. 'one should look for a companion, a friend to share thoughts with, equal ...'

'That's fine,' Acel cut him off. 'But I'm not sure that is what people originally look for in a mate. Maybe it develops, how would I know? I'm a TransmuCast kid.'

Acel knew he himself was not simply going back to live in the Dome with his mother again of course, if he ever would be able to; though that is what he most wanted to do, to return to a regular life as before, only wiser and happier. He had something to do first, something that he could not explain to Church or to anyone else alive ... except maybe the strange and violent man responsible for the obstacle which he must remove at all costs. Was this a crazy idea? It would be crazy not to, even if it was a crazy idea. The most beautiful experience of his adult life surpassed any loyalty he felt toward returning immediately to the stagnation of endless little worries about paying for endless use of TransmuCast and all the masturbation that was consumed in it.

'Are you going back to see your wife right away, Church?' Acel risked asking one afternoon in a long series of long days in which the weather had become warmer; they were descending and had glimpsed patch after patch of green under their feet.

'Maybe I should ...' Church's accent continued to play tricks.

'But what?'

'Women are so very charming, Acel. But maybe they are a waste of time.'

'How can you of all people say that? I don't know how you can think that way! After you forced me to listen to you moan and groan, after you moaned and groaned for months about punishing yourself and confession and riddling yourself with condemnation—Now you're finally set free to make amends and pick up the thread.'

'Maybe that's exactly why, Acel. It's development.' Church added with a satisfied nod behind his tinted glasses.

'Devil—hope—what was that?'

'Look, Acel. Everything you're saying, sometimes I feel I've gone to far. No way out of the TransmuCast, you know? Overwhelming my mind. This religion of romantic love everyone's so addicted to. The songs, the fantasies, the TransmuCast legends, programmed roses filling the breath in ecstasy ... I not sure if I should have so much faith in it. But ... am I capable of stopping it, of stepping out of it?'

'Well, just because something's popular that doesn't mean it's automatically wrong, Church. There is some good in it or it wouldn't be what it was.

We've all indulged in it in a TransmuCast game at least once. But passions have to be tamed with reason. You have to tame them somehow as you would an animal servant ...'

'I know. I know all about hard work. One thing which I feel I've learned being out here and walking in the snow with you, talking with you as we walk behind those Outland queers, and seeing the whole beautiful world here,' Church stopped and stamped his feet in the crush. He turned his face to Acel, eyes a green mirror at him. 'If you can't change your personal life, what is the worth of all your suffering?'

'That's true,' Acel admitted cautiously. He was thinking that this worth might depend on *how* someone changed their life, and he couldn't guess how Church was going to change his.

V

Where is she now? Still fading out of touch, through silver curtains, running, out of the touch that once but briefly held communion with every soul in the mortal empire of our world. Acel-Rice was almost oblivious to her location with his hand swimming in the most powerful substance on Earth. But the secrets were pink and gelatinous. Despite how he'd known her and the enchantment he'd felt in a previous life, she was a mystery to him who'd known her only in this life's childhood and never once again since.

But she was an agony to him who had. Yes, the pained one ... pining ... searching for his lost empire. Acel-Rice felt *him* clearly.

What is she doing now? She had crossed the bright river, its colors scintillated over her across her thighs as she leapt over it. Crowds were waiting for her there. They had seen her burning over the plain like a goddess. The crowd, that people, they had been waiting for an answer since the TransmuDream implosion. They were a lost people, isolated. The rest is vague.

VI

Many days later Acel discovered that the snowy hills of the Outlanders existed on a vast frozen plateau. When they had begun to reach its edge Church proliferately cursed the uphill journey that he'd had to make as a prisoner in the opposite direction many months before. This led him to cussing their guides again too. Acel wondered if this was part of Church changing his personal life.

After a full day of descending a steep little path along sheer rock sides, to where there was no more snow and the surrounding hills became softer, they began to have glimpses of something different beyond them. It looked like a black and flat plain, painted and glimmering out to the horizon. Acel wondered if was the sea he'd always wanted to visit. Yana, when asked, only said that it was not water and that the Dome was just beyond it. Indeed in the clearest moments of day there could be seen the faintest outline of a great shimmering on the horizon. The Dome from outside, a sight neither Church nor Acel had really seen with decent perspective; a very exciting possibility. Acel expected Church to go in search of his wife when they came near it, no matter what he said to the contrary. But as for himself, he had no idea … If Venus wasn't there, where was he? Again, Acel felt torn between returning home and continuing life on another consistent impulse from inside.

It might be mentioned as an aside in this report that the nights Acel and Church traveled with the Outlander band were more bizarre than the days before they slept. A fire was made, rough dried meals with millet porridge eaten, or occasionally some small animals their guides had hunted; the Outlanders on one side speaking low among themselves, Acel and Church on the other, generally quiet with Church glowering across the no man's land. The feelings evident on his face were intensified on occasions when Yana, acting as if on a dare, scooted up closer to Acel with strange soft questions about their destination, the assurity of their cure, or the life beyond them.

'Do you have a Cube in your Dome?'

'What?" Church scoffed. "What for? We have Cones!'

Acel waved his hand. 'No, we don't, Yana. Your people are very special and very lucky. But I think you have carried your Cube—'

'Yes, we carried it on a pallet. With a luxurious covering. No one was permitted to touch it. The elders of the Council always walked beside it. Long before I was born.'

'Not so long.' Acel chuckled.

'Why do you laugh, Doctor?'

'Your story reminds me of an older story I've read in an old book, about a people's migration. They too had a Cube.'

'What kind of a book is that? A manual?' Church asked.

'It was a book of religion. Religion like we have in the Dome. But in older times, before TransmuDream, people had no TransmuCast, only religion. That's what they clung to day and night. There were many religions in the world, and all together they might describe a portrait of the human soul. The problem is, the peoples of the different religions didn't care about that and they couldn't get along. They were always trying to prove to each other whose was better. They fought savage wars over this.'

'Wars? Sad ... Ah, but still I guess I see how it could happen,' Church said glaring at the Outsiders. 'But what you said, and have said to me before, Acel, is ... beautiful.'

Yana giggled and crept back to tell his comrades what he had heard.

'I don't trust those Outlanders,' Church muttered.

'I know, Church, I know.'

Night after night a very similar episode was enacted.

'What do people *do* in the Dome, Doctor?' Yana would inch over and ask.

'Make babies, Numbnut,' Church rumbled.

Not a tremor passed over Yana's face. He remained gazing at Church and Acel until the silence became gross.

'They're doing less of that nowadays,' Acel said sympathetically. 'They go to their jobs. Eat crummy lunches. Attack each other with futile mindsex in the street. Get home as soon as possible and plug themselves into the TransmuCast.'

'Maybe they haven't spent as long in a cage as I have, or you.'

'Or as long in the snow,' Yana said hollowly.

'You pity yourselves more easily than another,' Church spat out.

'Your conscience is clean now, Mister Church? That's not how you complained to us for nine months.'

'You bastard parasite!'

Acel often felt he had to stop these arguments, he always did. Perhaps Yana was genuinely curious, and Church was genuinely resentful.

'Self-preservation is all grown in, even with conscience, Yana,' he said. 'Church, isn't it a good idea then to imagine a proper duty of conscience?'

Another amelioration. And still the distance and cold hatred growing every night and day as they pushed forward; Church's temper ever more delicate, his behavior more erratic.

All the while Acel becoming stronger, in body, in spirit. Certainly there were enough pains during this journey. But as Church became more erratic, Acel learned to check and keep in line the histrionics of his own body's whelpings with each uncomfortable hour in the wilderness. Rather than just going along with its every cowardly mew. The beginning of his second level of maturity.

Finally the morning came when they reached the black lava plains that Acel had glimpsed more often as they'd made their way down. Vast, shimmering— it *was* like a sea, an impenetrable sea of Hades. But it wasn't the only surface of the Earth black-stained that could be seen from the dead eyes of the moon. An alien observer able to peer down through flashing toxic neon cumulus would've noticed frequent volcanic landscapes and the occasional red pit-point of their glowing origin. Places of frozen rock vomited from our shrunken planet's wounds during its rough reconstruction after TransmuDream's implosion and the resulting new world, which didn't last long before irrupting with rebellious gods offended with human manipulations at last. The Rangers in those days only had to bend Space backwards in Time to regain the semblance of our planet at all, the one Acel now walked on. The group had made their way down the hills streaming with clear cold creeks and now stood on broken rocks and steaming wet black shoal gazing at the lifeless field they must cross toward the Dome, heated in the refracted sun.

Church stood alone talking to himself . Or rather, he'd been talking to Acel the whole time, as he was doing increasingly, reliving his folly and muttering spitted words. He had merely diverted off and was speaking to the sky now.

'Oh, I know now why I did it, I know why. Because I'm a sex machine. I'm a sex machine.' He lifted his hand beseeching the air. 'Oh, thank you, God! You have made a sex machine! You're so smart!'

Acel glanced around the lava plain once more and at the constant display of electrical dissonance high above them. He looked back at the huge teeth-ridge of snowy wall they'd come through, miraculous and immense behind them. He suggested Church relax and have something to eat.

'That's right. I should relax. Maybe I should. Got to preserve the health. It's all we've got. You do everything for what you care for and then you die.' Once more he turned to the sky. 'Oh! Thank you, God! You have made a complex life, people we care about and love us, and then you make us die. You're so smart!'

Acel smiled briefly. Church posing against the universe with his glasses and moustache. He was obviously heading toward some form of crises and decision as they neared his home. This kind of sarcasm reminded him of Mr Venus. Suddenly the thought occurred to him with the force of a Megalopolitan bus. But not a thought, a feeling of awareness like someone watching you from behind. The nameless one through the Cube reaching out, probing wire-like dark fingers of mind. Would these invasions last forever? Invasions, or remembrances? Acel made a gesture shrugging it off. He knew where Venus was and he would go down to tell Yana to amend their course northward to catch him there.

Suddenly a tremendous flock of tiny birds flew by overhead, covering the sky for long moments before they spiraled away. Acel and Church stood awed— they had never seen so many, it was amazing and hysterical, marvelous how they all went densely together away.

After a moment Church returned to his soft sneering, 'What's the difference between me and them? Impulses ... You're really smart ... Really smart.'

VII

A black horizon under a mauve dawn. Waves of heat disguised thin threads pointing at the heavens, waving as in wind or underwater. For a month now the group had traveled nights to avoid the naked heat, skirting the hills for water and small game northward, until Acel pushed them in, into the vast black broken plain of frozen lava. For several days now they had camped in these phantasmagoric surfaces, even more strictly rationing their food and water, sleeping on biting rock that alternated blazing or freezing between a day and a night. And one morning in the dim light, there they were. The strange wavering reeds scattered in the distance. After two days of this unceasing mirage the journeyers still had no idea what they were.

The state of Church's mind became of more concern to Acel after they'd turned north and progressed much farther than it would have taken to reach the Dome had they just kept on westward. Yana and his Outlanders had informed them of this many times; they complained of losing the way, the rare stars, the faintly visible rim of the moon by which they navigated. They too obviously felt distressed leaving away from their usual path to and from the great Dome to capture those potent and unlucky victims unfortunate enough to have strayed far from the Outskirts on the wrong day. This had given rise to peculiar legends in Church's Area of the Dome. But it had gone on for generations now. Lately, as more men braved the outside hunting further sustenance, the harvest had been rich. Church had seen many come and come and go and go from his little penitent's cage; his disdain growing into weird branches of repressed hatred.

Church followed in a zigzag fashion. Sometimes he muttered to himself incessantly. Other times he was silent with a look of stone frozen, and had to be called to his senses to catch up stumbling in the dark, which he did sheepishly flashing rueful glances at their Outlander guides.

Acel was sick of talking with him, and he had other things on his mind, especially the morning those mysterious obelisks came into sight. Once it became clear what they were, no one could offer an explanation. And every morning before sleep they stood staring at those strange towers scattered over low stepped plateaus, pristine and ominous, every step less distant. They were driving Church crazy, but so was everything. Worse, the Outlanders were growing increasingly restless before them, but Acel drove them on with words just short of promises.

Finally the early morning came when they were entering amongst these silent fanglike obelisks that coldly fingered the dark and livid sky. Each one fifteen meters high, and sheer black, they stood around in an obscure pattern, tall, monstrous artificial stalagmites grown from the harsh lava stepped floes. Slit windows were glimpsed near their erect tips. The awful smell of rotting flesh invaded their nostrils as they entered the weird periphery.

Yana ahead of them all yelled out and pointed toward something nearby. The others came running down the wide jagged steps and stopped short. A pungent odor of revolting decay filled the air.

A shock of lightning lit the plain unnaturally bright. Laying stretched out with his arms embracing one of the weird towers a large bodied man covered in his own noxious filth and severely burnt by the ill invisible sun of shrunken Earth's degenerate ozone. Acel gasped.

'He's alive!' Acel shouted and directed Yana to give the sick man water and nourishment.

'What's that?' Church asked when he came up. Acel ignored him staring amazed and piteous at the prostrate man who could barely take any of the water drops offered him. They all looked down at this for a while.

'I know him, Church. His is a life worth saving and which needs saving more than either of us. He is a murderer and a genius and a visionary. He may be a bad man, but he is no longer dangerous.'

'Maybe you told me about him before,' Church answered gravely.

'I didn't think you were listening.'

Church looked up at the towers. 'Do you smell that, Acel? I think your friend is worse than you know. Finishing him off now would be best.'

'Worse than beasts—'

'No, best!' Church shouted past his limit with these misunderstandings. He seized a long spear from one of the Outlanders, but they restrained him in an ugly struggle before he could use it on Venus's helpless body.

'Pity myself I may!' Church said with unexpected ferocity. 'But not that *thing*.' He lunged again at the prostrated man.

'Look at the low brow, the heavy jaw, the rough physic like steel corners. It's barely human. It has no place in our civilization!'

'What civilization, Church?' Acel looked up trying to calm him. 'Sedately paralyzed before the TransmuCast?'

'You think it's a joke? What do you think your damn HomeGuardsmen *do*? I've seen criminality in all its strains. You've only seen what you wanted to in a TransmuCast fantasy life. A brief walk from your little job was too much for you, before you had to lose it again in your TC or—what? a book, for God's sake! But the scum of the Outskirts and Outlands are creeping in the night, assaulting families while they lay paralyzed amused in oblivion. There are desperate wolves among the sheep. Don't you remember the Thumberto case, how much exposure did that get? That was from my Area, just before these impotent insects kidnapped me. A couple had woken up from TC to find their three daughters, ages eight to twelve, had been sexually abused in every way and dismembered all around the house seven days before. I remember the mother rushed out onto the road beating herself screaming, "Oh my God! Where am I? Oh my God!" She had to be restrained with force by four guardsmen. The father, too; he wanted to go back and switch on his fantasy again. Would they have spent all that time indulging themselves in solitary dreams if they'd known that was going to happen? How precious the days would have been. I ask you, who *can* sleep and dream contentedly knowing such things go on among us? And knowing one may have the power to prevent it, if one was simply more vigilant. But we do sleep, Acel, sleep we do. I hate and abhor crime in its every variety! I hate it in myself, I hate in others less interested in defeating than I am. I hate it in my love for my wife. That's *my* conscience, you sterile worms! Another thing you don't have that makes me a man … It goes on always in our Dome, Acel, in the night, in the Outskirt streets, in the quiet minds. The criminal vanity of acting on a brain impulse like it was an official edict.. Then you got these Outlander murderers acting on their pompous edicts like a natural impulse. Subhumans! The criminal is a flawed specimen, Acel, it doesn't blend with society—a weak link! It never matures, that's one thing. It's an overgrown child, vicious and selfish and, and totally careless. Its intelligence that awes you into thinking there's a heart—that's just the gnawing of a rat trying to get at everything you own. Sure, you can spare this beast if you want to.'

'You've never forgiven yourself, Church, it makes this hatred burn you, burn you perpetually—'

'You've told me all I need to know, the things you know he's done. I've known him all my life, maybe that's what I'm telling you. All my job anyway. The scum! Worse than a beast, he's a parasite. *Your* kind!' Church struggled against the Outlanders' hold. 'No animal would indulge in the cruelties his subspecies do just for fun! I used to deal with that kind of scum when I was in the HomeGuard, and let me tell you a sad fact: he's not original. An enemy within; watch your back; a killer in the home. Don't look now. He is the enemy of our species, man!'

Acel kept his mouth shut and paused quietly. It took some puzzling to understand through that horrible furious accent. The Outlanders hovered around gripping Church, gripping their pointed lances, something inside their very restraint of him urging revenge on a specimen of priapic vitality while he was down. But Venus was a broken man now, and the stench of the towers hung over him.

'Individuals woven into reactive patterns and bureaucratic systems of body and collective bodies—'

'What the hell are you talking about, Acel?' Church yelled.

Acel had been almost unaware that he was talking to anyone. He knew that Church was finally breaking. He started again.

'Let it roll past us, Church. He is not the Enemy. He is an obstacle. That's all. The true adversary wears too many masks to name.'

Church spat and fumed. His glasses were all awry on his head and his eyes shifted with helpless rage.

'Well, I can think of a lot of names! It's written all over him, a typical Renegade—'

The Outlanders jumped at a word which to them was nearly an identity— even while they had become such cloistered and petrified community themselves. They too had their weird vanities.

'Don't get your peckers up,' Church retorted. 'Maybe I only talk from my perspective, like you.'

'Look at him, Acel,' he continued, pointing down. His low voice broke fiercely. 'You get to be a certain age. And there's no mistaking the life of vanity and greed that you've led. All the disappointed passions of a life. They're all in a face by then. Can they get smoothed out or refined into something still attractive? Or does your face repulse your neighbors, who lie to you in half-words and enjoy destroying your name later? They get uglier themselves, so what? You've seen too much, as any HomeGuardsman in our great Dome has. Your eyes have seen too much pain. Your eyes have seen so much; the sufferings of *one* human at least. Anyhow, life by this age of you. One who cries while standing in public places. Your eyes are filled with sadness, yet dried by so much grief; they still live, but petrified. They still live with a raging angry brutal blood that must fill their sorrowful filaments, because you live and you must!'

Church in fact was weeping as he spoke.

'There is no fear anymore—only grief and cunning!'

Acel rushed to put his hand on him but had little to say. He pulled Church away from the terrible towers. The only thing he could think of uttering was a strange phrase from one of the old books in the Cube's chamber, 'Let sleeping dogs lie.'

He told the Outlanders to watch him there and headed back to Yana and Venus.

The burnt and dehydrated man wasn't much better off than from when they'd discovered him. Tiny flies crawled over his skin. But Acel steeled himself to his duty.

'Venus … Venus, can you hear me? Where is it? Is it near here?'

Acel must've asked the same questions a dozen times before Venus finally croaked out an inchoate sound. The sun continued to beat on them regardless of the cloth Yana was trying to stretch over their heads. In the distance Acel also heard the screams of Church on a new tangent. This was futile.

Acel stood and looked around. He noticed the proximity of Church to the tower and the position they'd found him in, on his stomach with his arms as if embracing it. A thin knotted rope of sheets hung some ways from its window. Obvious what had happened. Could it be up there? Among what else, Acel wondered, curling his nose at the horrid stench in the air.

Feeling hot and lightheaded Acel walked around between the thin obelisks, circling this way and that. Rolling kettle-drumming the distant thunder above seemed to reassure him. After a while he found what he thought he'd been looking for, flat in the lava surface. A normal Dome man could not have opened it, much less discovered it, nor could any display of mere brute strength, without unfortunate consequences. But there was a cunning in Venus's mind that Acel could now decipher easily. A standard old Ranger code: Emphaxis. It should not be revealed in this book.

A ladder led down deeply from the trap. At last Acel reached bottom. The aperture above was a small bright blaze.

VIII

Acel found himself in an ovular chamber. There was just enough illumination to see two passages leading off in almost opposite directions. Acel chose the one towards the tower where Venus lay above.

It wound about and many branches interrupted its progress. Acel could only decide through intuition which way to go. If intuition is how he could describe his decisions responding to the same pressure which led him northward to these hideous obelisks. He felt his way in the darkness with a hand along the smooth black lava wall. The silence and the tunnel were oppressive and he grew impatient.

Finally he found the ladder which he knew led up to the right tower. Acel was breathing in gulps. He climbed up to a landing from which he took a narrow spiral stair. This is it, he thought.

A locked door. It took him at least another half hour in the darkness before he discovered the next code that opened it, a combination of several old codes in a way, which should be forbidden. May the opportunity never present itself for this to be reported in person, but not otherwise. It would not be healthy for you to invest so much time in such abstract dreams of anonymous yearning.

'This little room,' Acel realized. 'is where she lived, where, she grew up.' The psychic traces of Krystal Elioud were too huge to ignore now. He did not know, could not imagine, how she came to have lived here, but it was unmistakable. The room was cooled with some discreet system and scattered with a woman's little possessions. The bed smelled of her body ... Diona's body ...

mingled hideously with the brute downstairs ... at many ages ... There was no doubt that it was her. Pictures she had drawn decorated the walls, insane pictures of scenes only Acel could understand immediately. They were of no earthly birth and no Dome child had ever possessed such dreams of passion and abandonment. Acel marveled at them in admiration and terror. The closest things he could relate them too, that were done by human hand, were those old books ... those old books he'd come across so rarely in his life, and so copiously in the chamber of the Gelatinous Cube.

A sound made him turn. In the doorway stood someone, something Acel had never wished to see again: the Red Duke.

'I owe you my gratitude for guiding me to this sentimental location, Sub-lieutenant Rice,' the Duke spoke sliding into the room. 'How could I, or my dear brother Lustos, have ever found such a treasure without you is beyond me.'

'It was Captain Rice when I embarked,' Acel answered, his voice failing as he tried to recall the courage with which he had once witnessed Sir Venus confront this terrible and alluring creature.

'Was it? So your masters have changed and your soul has changed hands ... many times.'

'While your master has always stayed the same: the Enemy—'

'Not so fast, Captain. Not so fast. You are an impatient, judgmental species, aren't you? Is it so impossible to believe that Desyristos has his own agenda in the world of your origin? Along with my brother as well? That we have our own plan and destiny? Is it so impossible to believe, given the incessant manifestations of your kind, who dote on us so, even now, even in their stagnation? Listen to their bodies yearn in their boredom and their stifling Dome. Ask yourself how it is that we, twins issued from the Venerable Beatrix, still travel freely here, doing whatever we may. You, too, little Acel, with your extraordinary interest in books and reports, you are not unknown to me. Your evident thirst for knowledge, real knowledge not superficial, has so often impressed me, called to me in your young age. A delight. The idea that we could collaborate and inform each other has occurred to me. Haven't we already? I remember the night not so long ago that you took that beautiful female to her room and did the things your natures intended you to do. I recall your joy in discovering your real emotions. Your vow that you would finally satisfy yourself by repeating them as often as you could. There is so much we could acquire from each other, Acel, and I am at your service.'

The heat from the Red Duke's body was overpowering and Acel could not but grimace fixedly staring at this diaphanous magnetic visage of pink and deep vermilion shades.

'It was fun,' Acel croaked.

'I daresay it was a lot of fun. Yes, we will have a long friendship. Your memories are succulent and they please me, so far as they persist. They do persist. That's one thing I can count on with your people, and especially those of you with such intelligence.'

'I think ...' Acel struggled to say. 'I think you are better off now than ever with humans trapped in the Dome.'

'Am I more satisfied? Ah, steadily but meagerly. What Domes within Domes your species has constructed to your purpose and mine. Delectable species. It always pleases you to futilely yearn with such secret vanity for those pleasures that you never allow yourselves. A delight, as I mentioned. But the present entertainment technology there—Transmu, Transmo, whatever it is—it shrugs off most inhibitions in a computerized dreamscape (though their fantasies are petty anyway) and we are left with the appetizer but not the meal. Am I content? No, not yet. Like you, not wholly fulfilled.'

Acel fell to the floor under the livid pressure of this terrible personality.

'You ask too much of us, Duke, your Grace.'

A laugh like the ripple of electric flames circled the room.

'Yes, I am of the old school, an old heritage. We have derived so much nourishment from your active little race. Before the implosions that have left your planet as it is, shrunken and underpopulated, what a variety of frustration I used to revel in. And more religions just kept springing up! A cornucopia. That's why I thought it was high time to make your acquaintance, face to face, *Doctor*.'

'Why'd you call me that?'

'Why, isn't that what those pathetic SnowPeople call you? What do they believe you can do for them—something so dear—restore their manhood, is it? Pause a spell … Imagine what you could do, with your new knowledge of the world and the world behind the world, with the whole human race at your beck and call for a lifetime? At this moment as we speak they are preparing to leave their barren Dome for a better life. They need direction.'

Acel's head was spinning. He leaned back on his knees with a hand bracing him on the floor. "Could it be, could it really be …?' he thought.

'You know why I've come here?' Acel stammered.

'Of course, Captain Rice. You forget that I have been involved with your species far longer than you have. Indeed, you can see the signature of Desire, my name, written throughout the ocean's depths to the mansions of space! You came here, as any of you would, searching for your lost playmate. The directions of sunlight that made her child smile so alluring. The mystery below your mind guiding you to her. The belief, not unfounded, that you were meant to be together. Just like every other *man*, your acidic juices pushing you around, the juices that taste so good to us. Your only difference is the memory of a past life that fuels your hopes—whereas the others all feed on the fumes of their internal combustion. In fact I'm a bit surprised that you haven't finished off your rival while he lays at your mercy. Seems to be common practice. Your friend the policeman had the same idea for another reason ... Interesting morsel, that one ... But I suppose a human heart softened in one direction is often soft in other directions.'

Acel stood up slowly, as deceptively as he could. His mission was safe. His mission ...

Red Desyristos prated on, 'Yes, your Dome upbringing—how rich in delights it is!—really stunts your sexual maturity, doesn't it? No natural outlets since the onset of puberty. Your sexual maturation is halted in adolescence, it atrophies, and you are left in a whirlpool of frustrated embryonic little yearnings that I find so consistently nourishing. Grown bodies with half-brains clogged with violent desire that addicts you to your tedious irresistible masturbations, living and striving in inescapable hotpink bubbles—sealed with an erotic scar. That's all you have. A computer stroking your plastic mind while your body wilts raging in bedsores and unexercised necrosity. Less and less capability of joy's efforts, in TransmuCast or out of it. A single-minded yearning microbe. No wonder a specimen like you would travel half the globe to find a dream of childhood infatuation. No wonder at all. Losing your head like this. What's reality to you but pain?' The Duke laughed.

'What you say may be true,' Acel stalled. 'What do you want with me now?'

'*May* be? Look into my eyes, boy!'

Two bright hotpink gems gleamed and melded together in a viscous sphere that caused Acel to sigh in successive throbbings. It was a sphere or it was an endless slippering hole pulsating and attracting in starving contractions. Its livid wet walls formed myriad details of fleshy cities, protuberances and articulate rows of slick manipulable edifices trembling pink in myriad passageways amongst a myriad populace of hot dreams. Foam slid down slopes as districts convulsed. The yelpings of multitudinous tongues blended together in a wailing scream while the city oozed sweat of salty colors. Distant, not far from the edge, an ornate palace yearned outward in gleaming hotpink bonds.

'Such is Hermosa, Land of Smile, as it was and as it exists beneath the servitude of your race. Dry now, anonymous, her empress vanished, awaiting her heirs and existing only in my memory. Yes, fed only with frugal dishes from only one unreligious planet now.'

The Duke had closed his eyes and Acel still stared at his sheer crimson face carved of sad rubiate stone.

'You have the power to transmit, Captain Rice. Isn't the world I have shown you far fairer than the dirty little gropings of a people lost in radioactive sand? Make sure your people do not alter their traditions insofar as Hermosa cannot remain aloof. Sacredize us. Protect us. We can grow as an obsession throughout the galaxy as we once were. And not merely sustained as an unspoken vice among dilapidated pleasure addicts!'

The brilliant eyes were open once more.

'You are the new leader. With the Cosmic Rangers on our side, protecting love against destruction, we can rule the universe with a new religion!'

Acel's own eyes were darting around inside his head.

The Duke suggested, 'Even these appetizingly sterile Snowmen are off to a holy start ...' but Acel did not want to listen. Not unless by some by some word or attitude he could deceive the ruthless prince into believing that he agreed, in order to buy time enough to find what he was after and get away with it.

'Whatever are you doing now?'

'Oh?' Acel had begun strolling about the room with his fingers on his chin. 'I'm just considering if impotence *is* a good start, from what I know of human nature, great Duke.'

Acel glanced at the reeking bed—disgusting. He tried to spy under it. He took in the shelves. Nothing. The rope of sheets tied to the awry dresser. He wandered over to the closet wardrobe.

'A very grand start, I should say, if it's canonized,' the Duke was saying whilst jotting notes in a flaming notebook.

Where would that lonely villain hide such a thing? What did it look like? What would such an audacious man do?

Acel opened the wardrobe and pushed his hands through the silken gowns.

'Looking for a token of her affection?'

Acel froze, and continued casually.

'A small indulgence, your Grace.' It was difficult enough to converse with this awesome being without trembling, but an amorphous and pathetic rage was swelling in him too, much like he'd felt in the Cube. Did all the ancient forces of the galaxy believe they could just come here and push humans around with their moral plans, their consciences, their new religions? He knew that he wasn't considering fairly so many of the individuals, his ex-colleagues in another lifetime whom he once loved—like a beautiful dream—they had helped at the same time to preserve and protect his race, his family. And Venus, too, once upon a time had been one of them before Captain Rice's commission … Even Venus … Was this all a game concerned with power over his pawnlike species, over himself? Acel grimaced and tightened his fists. Maybe he should make Venus both pay for his crimes *and* tell him what he wanted to know.

At that moment a black form slipped into the chamber, worse and darker than a shadow. Features and raiment identical to the horrific Red Duke, but a color lustrous and fetid like decomposing polished obsidian—Lustos, his gruesome twin. Acel leapt back against the wardrobe doors. Wordlessly he flowed in, nostrils dilated, quivering and craning toward the stripped mattress's obscene odor. On all fours he touched toward it like a cat—and drew back puzzled and finally with a quick dumbfounded expression across his ebony face that Acel didn't miss. Lustos looked up at his brother.

'Stop sniffing around down there! Control yourself, darling twin of me. Better yet, let's leave this boy to do his own last sniffing here before he joins us out. You can't imagine how tedious dialogue with one of these creatures can be. What do you say we go down to the base and amuse our old acquaintance in his wasted state, while this one masturbates in his lost love's underwear, or whatever it is they do—his exhalations will mingle with the other's downstairs—exquisite symphony. Pity there aren't more weakened or extreme humans around. Maybe the Snowdwellers will do.'

Lustos leapt up, very happy with the suggestion, and followed his twin down the spiral.

'Don't keep us long, Captain—er, Doctor!' Desyristos's arrogant invitation wound back up.

As soon as they were gone Acel leapt on the mattress and began to feel around. Cool and very soft, but very bare. A stranger smell was coming from it though than he'd expected. Quickly Acel jumped and searched around the dresser. He came back with a pair of scissors and began stabbing and cutting away, pulling out the downy stuffing. This was getting to be hard work. Suddenly an idea occurred to him and he called himself foolish.

He stepped back and pushed the mattress up off its frame. There it was. A large black fumigated briefcase in a boxlike section. Ridiculously easy, Acel smiled with his old wry grin of triumph.

He pulled it out and hugged it to his chest. This is how I begin the world. This is my key and my antidote. *I am untouchable!* Acel hopped and spun around with ecstasy.

Suddenly he stopped short.

Before him on the other side of the bed stood the silent loathsome Black Twin Lustos fawning and smiling, rotating his awful head side to side in a similar kind of pleasure that was repulsive and inspiring with the darkest joys.

Acel backed against the wardrobe. 'It's mine!' he cried. 'Keep away!'

The gruesome creature seemed to nod faintly in amusement or satisfaction and slipped out of the chamber in a prolonged archaic bow.

The feelings of disgust faded slowly, leaving Acel with a cold reflection. Where would he go now? Where would he start? And then he thought of those he had traveled here with. Church's pathetic and terrible damnation of Venus. Human words. But Acel could not believe it inevitable that everyone's soul be destroyed in time. He knew that his father's eyes never looked like that, like Church's then. No, they were lit by warmth and zany adventure. Eyes that loved life and had humor, whichever way it turned! Acel always remembered his father like that, until the old man had devoted himself to the TransmuCast, for a life which the Dome could never give people enough of. Acel understood that very well. But he was far away from any TransmuCast now, and what he held in his arms was ... greater. But his mother's pain drew him homeward. Was that where he should go?

Outside, he heard a cry. Were they torturing Venus, those monsters? Too many feelings erupted in him.

Acel ran to the door and down the long stair as fast as he could. He painstakingly made his way through the tunnels. Climbing the ladder took even longer with the heavy case.

'They won't have him if I can help it. He is *our* criminal. They wouldn't understand him ... or do they?'

Finally he flung himself out onto the hard hot lava and raced back to the tower's base.

There was no one there. Acel looked around wildly. He threw the cased Device down on the stone and jumped up and down on it. 'No, no, you stupid man, where have you gone, where have they taken you?' Of course no impression was made on it whatsoever.

'Church!' he screamed and ran toward where he'd last seen him—was he still here? Had they taken them all? Midway he turned and went back for the Device and then ran on again muttering desperately.

On the periphery of the obelisks' ring and saw the Snowmen laying pell-mell askew and dead with shocking wounds. This was more disorienting than anything he'd lived through in a vicarious TransmuCast, that was for sure. No Church. A couple of the Snowmen seemed to be still clinging to life, this was awful. Yana was among them, and Acel crouched down to him.

'Yana, darling Yana, it's alright. Where is Church?'

It was not alright and Yana only gurgled until he spat out a delirious whisper of blood.

'Demons took him, Doctor. The sick man ... ran away ... so strange ... he woke up, ran away ... They punished us. They flew away, away with Church. How can they all fly, so easy ... Make me better, Doctor ... Doctor!'

The Outlander said no more.

With tears in his eyes Acel ran in a direction he believed was toward the Dome, home. A pressure in his head made the weight of the case he was carrying immense, its handle burning like electricity in his hand.

'Leave me alone!' he yelled winded.

Suddenly he halted and crouched down in an instinct. The awful Twins were fighting over something flying away in the air.

'Rich treasure! What a conscience! What a catch!' they screamed. 'Mine! No, mine!'

Sounds and vicious whispering words of which war is too small a one to name. Tearing at each other with ignoble and intimate clawings in a copulatory embrace more like one trying to devour the other. They flew over his head and away, away into the livid cumulus ... begging one another's forgiveness in real supernatural sour tears as they continued to fly and rend unceasingly ...

Finally Acel came across the man, Church, laying on his back. He appeared unscathed but a deeper wound was killing him.

'Church! What happened? No, don't speak—'

'Give my love to her, Acel. She was kind to me in her way. I have been true to her in mine. Maybe it's funny how life works out, you know. I have learned there are more forces in this crazy world than all my reason ever reckoned on. What a strange nightmare I've just had, Acel. I wasn't trained for this! It was like my soul was a barren plain over which tornadoes of violent emotion ruled wildly, wandering where they would through my body. No, pulled through me! It was just a mirror of me, do you understand! Do you understand?'

Acel desperately checked his friend for wounds, for some way of helping him. One night in a cell facing extermination, endless days trudging together in terrible conditions, Acel realized now that he felt closer to Church than he had with any other man in his life. He was appreciating this too late.

'A mirror! A black face and a red face, laughing, laughing ... I listened, I learned ... I learned a thing or two about this old shell. They said I'd fill them up. One greedier than the other. They began lovingly, brotherlike, helping each other, lifting food into the other's mouth. But got snappier, quicker and slower. Accused one of giving smaller pieces. Arguing like dogs over my ventricle. That's how they flew off, with some piece of my heart between their yanking naked teeth!'

Acel could not comprehend some of Church's words in his accent slurring with exhaustion—no, not until later, when his mind could puzzle shot through with a later clarity ...

'Tell her I loved her. I still do. Do go and tell her, a message in her new life, just a note. It's impossible to think of them, you know, outside either pity or lust. If you want friendship, Acel, only men or some untouchable woman might do ... The woman you love, she is omnivorous, don't you see, and she devours the weaknesses you reveal to a friend. It's not the same. Not the same. Some manager of an intimate Business Cone, sensitive, but ... My sergeant was a man like that. He could get us to do ... You're a good friend, Acel, a good man.'

Acel believed his friend was delirious and tried to relax him. He caressed his brow and shhh'd him gently.

Long hours passed and entered the dusk. Church's words became only more abstract, less comprehensible, perhaps more meaningful or more stupid, but Acel cannot now transcribe them. The man's life then faded with the sunlight. In red wild colors of words for which there is only feeling and impression, then absence.

Frankfurt paced his mansion beaming. The plan was going well. 42% of the Dome was under Frankfurt's control and moving toward the Outskirts. 5% of the population has already evacuated and was colonizing the old irrigation system outside. Presently supplied by Frankfurt's monopoly of course. But once they had developed a sustainable agriculture, Frankfurt had a few other plans for their industry: machine parts, computer systems, everything short of TransmuCast, which he held in his own private reserve. Something they could aspire to as a promised heavenly dream of luxury, a memory and a promise … This he could use to his psychological advantage in maintaining power; Frankfurt knew quite a bit about managing people. Docile people, as he'd always known them. He had little interest in changing their characteristics much, men in his position never have had. It didn't matter that the actual fact of the matter was Frankfurt himself was far away from being able to supply anyone but his immediate circle with any kind of entertainment of that caliber anyway. Human society has always submitted to the swells of constraint and rebellion. It may, or may not have, in its dramatic history climbed upward with each manifestation … But it certainly has realized a variety of forms, of art on its measurably largest scale.

Acel stood. He walked back into the towers' pattern. Not private enough. He made his way again torturously up to the tower. A certain fear made his hands tremble, that the demonic Dukes would return—or almost worse, that Venus would, realizing that Acel was in possession of his precious life work.

Where had Venus gone to now? Ghastly person. Confounded personality. But dangerous, truly dangerous. The only answer was that he had gone in search of his lost favorite. Acel smiled wryly once more, wondering if this could be called an irony, that Venus was forsaking his desperate ambition, for a woman whom his pride had imprisoned and who had obviously fled from him. But it would be no laughing matter if Venus discovered Acel now.

Curious hermaphroditic-tetradic lock device. Several attempts using a variation on old themes only enabled him to defuse its fatal trap. He sat on the bed and pried open the briefcase with the same scissors he'd used before. A bizarre wiring system of old ammunition magazines, their hideous contents coursing back and forth between other little machines Acel could not decipher. It was all the work of evil genius. Acel had to force down his nausea. A pair of large wet headphones hung inside the lid. Acel put them on. A little spongy handle protruded straight out which was obviously the main control, saturated with the unspeakable juices. Without thinking, Acel grasped it.

The machine began to connect Acel first to the essential workings of nature ... He's an operator in a central station hierarchy—transported by his own haphazard connections—he flips tiny switches in experiment and colors are sprayed across the essential elements ... Squares, triangles, DNA ladders crawling through his skin ... like working on an incredible complex machine of almost intangible parts ... triangles and throbbing names of hierarchy stations crawling through his skin ... One could lose one's mind ... was losing it in surges of cosmic chariot speed, a minor sun slipping with the reins; liquid suns the reins slipping from his hands. Through his skin. Hitched to a falling star. Levels of too many reins this zany machine, Acel has to get on the right track. No, the plunging steed! The noise is almost painful; he's climbing through his blood's throbbing the only sense of time and space. It reminds him of an extreme TransmuCast ... but of a subject unsuitable for public consumption as it was, no society but the most spiritual relations could occur ... could endure this throbbing ... throbbing which brought images closer, closer. Those slithering fingers from eight different points are the Gelatinous Cubes ... driven by a Ranger probing in search of him or in search of this Device, to search and destroy ... He-Whose-Name-I-Do-Not-Know looking for the word he is looking for ... to search and destroy ... coming closer now with the scent of his body, the organization of his body's structure identified by that cube in Snowland. This is how we planned to do it. ... And now they're almost upon him ... "Come with us," steely voices of angels. "Learn the truth." Could Acel recognize them, dissuade them before they dismantled this Device he'd been sent to find, it would dismantle his mind ... ravaging his capacity for thought. In, out, in, out. Venus's scent all around his decisions, the obscene clearness of a tragic ego, like fingering the horrid man's brain in a grand pity of our species. This floating Device of twists, knots, shapes, vessels, lamps gleaming with accusation and ambition which only a living human could admit he knew. Acel did not want them to have this sapphire machine which was made by the hands of his species. But here they were. Forms of Alien Advisors horrifying the mind's eye and often with a melting ecstatic love; it would dismantle his mind ... the way they were picking at the propulsion system ... of the Device he was riding to enter into the center of the primal substance ... elusive substance ... slipping, slipping off, out, in, out, out, in, out of the periphery again. He understood that his sanity would be collateral damage in this mission of the Cosmic Rangers encroaching. Is this what he had volunteered for? Flaming termites gnawing his rationality. "Come with us." Acel began to withdraw from them in dread but he could not disengage from Venus's wrapping wheeled levers—He surely did not know how. Exit was entrance. He was a two-legged rat in a maze, a labyrinth with eight minotaurs pursuing, gaping gnawing sweet mouths. He began to scream and consider ways to shed his skin and leave himself behind to these angelic parasites.

Acel was pushed out of the way and slid across the floor. Sir Venus had returned and was taking the controls furiously, suddenly trying to connect with the Rangers.

"I have a report to give... a report!" Venus screamed pathetically and desperately trying to maintain the contact Acel had made...

Acel saw him shouting, "I am Arlequin Venus, 1st Sergeant, 3rd regiment, India company—Goddarn you, what are you doing to me ...' The headphones askew and sweat flying from his wound-covered body. 'You 're destroying my life's work ... not again ... not again ... Don't you understand? I have a report to give you ... my report ... my life!'

A moment of concentration.

Venus yanked off the headphones, leapt up and smashed his precious Device under his shining bleeding feet.

There was an immense silence which only poetry could describe. Acel's education had not given him the words to do it—he stared wild-eyed, astonished at such a man, a man like this.

Slowly Venus brought his heavy gaze to Acel. 'It is better to spend your life making your own device than to be just a cog in someone else's machine.'

Venus's expression changed to that of extreme sullen hatred. He trembled. And then to sullen sadness.

"Have I ever ...? Have I ... ever ... *ever* ... done something ... like this to you, to any of you? No. No ... No ... How could I do it, how could you be so weak? Maybe this time your kind have won. You were the sign of doom for me, both of you. You have taken away my joy, but you have not taken away my desire."

He turned to leave.

'Venus!' Acel calls out to him in an anguish he doesn't understand.

Venus turned back around. "Forgive me if I leave you to a world you claim to love. Expect me later ... or never. There is someone I am going to find. Something more important than all the plans in the universe now. I have nothing else, nothing else now but a passion even more ridiculous than my pride ... You idjit.'

Venus left.

I

Ages since the dusk had fallen. The twilight splashing its final attack of color across the world in tragedy and sweet, no, inspiring beauty. So relatively few of the Dome's denizens had ever witnessed it beyond the dull pink glow that flowed in a strange luminosity across that life long crystalline shelter. This new acquaintance with nature, even under a sick sky wrought with ionic cumulous, makes them obviously breathless with the beginnings of a new nascent devotion to the specie's reborn adventure of life.

Acel was some meters from the great Gate on a small rise of dirty sand. He watched the midnight flow of citizens migrating outward. HomeGuardsmen directing, checking ID's, directing. People with the possessions they could carry sadly and yet full of an unknown feeling, moving forward—temeritously on the verge of a pleasure our species had built itself for!

Acel was looking for his mother, his father, even old schoolmates. None yet. He had been to the old blockhouse, it was abandoned. The HomeGuardsmen he had asked were not trained to do anything but inquire his origin and send him on to some new area of colonized desert. That is where he would go tomorrow, to rejoin his family if they'd made it yet.

But another feeling made him enjoy gazing at this mass movement of people outward across the world. It was a great feeling, or he was on the verge of something great. And then there was another thought too, that given enough time, the old library he'd worked at, the old bookstore would be open to his pick and choice. Or would the owner think to bring that junk out here? He thought not. But those old books could not be abandoned. He kept puzzling a way to transport them, even if he was the only fool from the Dome doing so. Maybe people could learn to read them again, after all, in the wasteland they must conquer.

It is the middle of a long summer night. Standing in a valley made of dirty sand. Dead dry vineyards cover its faraway slope reaching up supplicating the void; rows of wizened dwarfs slowly blowing away in the dust of Time. Our people moving, spreading out, migrating with their intimate songs amongst the temporary structures punctuating a hard day's work. The sleep of children and soon to be dreamers, souls yet to be born alive in a new mortal empire. Below the distant masses of inky stars.

I will be going soon to send this last part of my reports, the conclusion of Deeply Privileged. Any one of those Cubes will do … No longer hidden from me. But they will remain hidden until … a later time.

I do not relax my discipline here, my masters, though you perceive me to hesitate. I am well aware that every thought I now have will be engraved in my report, fully visible to you—my character naked, made naked by how I have reflected my experience Deeply Privileged. I have reflected. Communicated without obstacle. That is the amazing thing about human life. You are personally responsible for how you react every moment. Every moment is mortal.

Even if it could be proven to us that we, our minds as only the Cosmic Rangers understand them, are not mortal, still we are bound by insoluble fraternity to ask why … Why? Why? Why our addictive and monstrous penchants, this appetite for deplorable cruelty to one's own kind; for breaking the body and spirit of anything presumptuous enough to resemble us; for slowly burning the innocents of every living age on an instinctual rack of periodic malice, more perverse than the most insentient of invertebrates; the contempt for oneself while Time itself tears us limb from limb—from that which one most cherishes: appalling design of things. Our masters have apparently seen fit to make us only intelligent enough to have to concentrate with all our brain's power just to realize life's daily horror and our congenital susceptibility to our Enemy; just to see that love and hate are two sides of the same heart. Could it not have been differently structured? This is all true enough to force you to stare deadening yourself at a sedating screen, so it has been. But you will soon see how I make sure that you will perceive something much other than a ghost imitating a ghost's appetites in your little pastime. Much better than further paralysis—we have indulged too long! unable to penetrate life. We now ask, How can we live, how *will* we live, in such a world? How can we love and not be destroyed by it?

My report—in this last page of churning milk—I have adjusted its frequency to thrive in every Cube and to find its way into every TransmuCast still vibrant, however long that survives; to vibrate in every human screen and electronic emanation; to beckon to minds across the world as I was once beckoned, drawing them nearer themselves; and to infiltrate the animated representations of the future, whatever technology comes. You will see what I have done. Those who do not like my answers to the question above as they came about during Deeply Privileged, or do not understand them yet, will at least never be able to ignore the question again. Yes, your future men may not be so surprised to find me near their minds when the book of reality's machinery is opened once more before their ever-blessed ever-curious eyes. Our mission's success, it's just beginning, a mere scratch of our Dome's surface born above our brains, for those elementary learners to take note of. And gather what they will of our mission, called by us an appropriate name.

My people, my brothers and sisters, I have just seen them again! Wheeling in the everpresent seas of thunder, the pair strangely brighter than falling stars, arcing with dangerous speed over the murky firmament of this world. Did you hear their speech together too, in the silence of these neglected fields just outside our archaic Dome? Hungry, snapping, weirdly loving sounds for which war is too small a word. That frightening play between opposite inter-dependent yearnings, ever seeking, imploring, ravenous, strengthening dangerously—still with us, still hovering around our hearts, their heated steeds, pulled behind, invisible, pervasive, plummeting and rising. Their cloaks blow wildly behind them like bats' wings of viciously opposed colors, spiralizing around their prey and their idol. These old gods can not forget me, nor you, their true and destined masters. They are twins, polar, rhythmic, tangible—I have revealed their secrets to you and you will be able to train them in a way that suits you. You can call to them with every art you know, from every angle. They are not too distant to serve you, reborn, reborn. Ah!

Come outside of your Dome now, you are coming. Coming as men and women together in the newest ways. Take a beloved fistful of our precious Earth's sand. Stand in the secrets of our world. Write us a letter in the endeavor.

[That's the way of Captain Rice's last report, from *Deeply Privileged*. Of course, your Excellency, there was some following mumble and jumble surrounding the end of his connection, apparently having to do with his journey by motorcycle to at least one of the hidden Cubes in order to send this, but we don't have much frame of reference for it. He seems to have located the others, and has kept the coordinates as cryptic as we would like, somewhere in his work, whatever that means. The report was obviously sent in more than one stage. He had already mastered at some point isolating the preferred texts for his readers' consumption. A high work of art no less, seen from the Human view. And that is who he intended it for, he says so himself.

Hero or Renegade? His report begs the question now, doesn't it? Yes, our Rice has become rather adept on that little world of his origin. One wonders if even my present commentary will be included in that last promise of universal distribution, if he has the skill by now to do that; he had at one time; we have no way of knowing until his intention, carried out, is reflected somewhere in there. There is some danger in him doing this maybe, as long as our Enemy's minions hang their glistening tongues out into the mist between worlds listening for the weaknesses they thrive on. This depends on how insecure our communications are made by him, and ultimately how vulnerable this vigilante effort makes himself. A species like that comprehending the history of our monitoring and supporting them, as they used to—Is such a revelation even useful to them? Rice may think so. He is their specialist, not I.

Nothing further has been traced from him. It is speculated that he has rejoined his family as Acel Daniel in their new colony life. Such are the foundations of a Human mind. Your Excellency, you will remember that I have recommended him for a high commendation. It may be argued at the inevitable tribunal that his actions which eventually led to the success of *Deeply Privileged* were a collection of serendipity, accidents of passion and circumstance. That's hard to disagree with by our positive logic. But I beg you to consider the nature of his species, the height of their reason which allows them to believe they are, as he says, 'only intelligent enough to have to strive with all our concentration just to realize life's horror ...' Poor things, who've always been both far too susceptible to love's Enemy as well as being the field of love's most complex manifestations. Their nature loses us. We find that despite the most concentrated will available to a man, by and large it would never appear to be more than a madness to us. The issue than is, when the knowledge of our awareness flooded him, and offended his self-image, did he not do what could only be expected of the best of his kind—and therefore succeed?

His nemesis occurs. Venus, Arlequin Venus, the rogue Ranger and Renegade anti-historic human whose murderous unreflective vanity provided the excuse for Deeply Privileged in the first place. His childish Device reaching for everlasting power—on Earth and here—over the agents of his disgrace and punishment. Hideous anthropomancy, slavery, illegal executions of his former staff, the obstacle to and perversion of our high reason. An ape of a Ranger. I say let the humans deal with him. His innumerable crimes were against them, ultimately. With this frightening pinnacle of valor and conceit demonstrated to their development after so much effort, is it any wonder not only that they live in a submissive herd, but that they are unhappy doing so and yet continue to do so? Not surprisingly, Captain Rice's report emphasizes that it is their nature to arbitrate their own comprehension of mercy. We may yet find that heroic and stupid soul useful to us once again. If your Excellency deigns to understand what is meant by 'useful' in terms of our human charges, this indefatigable species that has exhausted all of us with their dangerous periods of activity and inactivity. Forgive my frankness, and let us assume that our communication is still secure (in that it will not be figured out by its subjects, bless them).

This Arlequin Venus now resides with his lady—yes, Krystal Elioud—in some backwater of primitives. I neglect her assigned legend under the mission we are discussing, no longer important. She played the effective role necessary to the downfall of a man of Venus's stature—that is, she softened him and made him more irrational. A very good choice, if I may say so. Rice discovered that she is a descendent of the notorious Nephilim, as we knew, and her charms were well suited to the mission. There is enough evidence for this. But we must also consider her a casualty of the operation as she has never come to terms with Deeply Privileged, not yet ... And her existence becomes more mysterious at every page of this story. How much a part did she play in his abominable alchemistic Device? We think about where it was found anyway—perhaps Rice discovered some signs of a psycho-sexual ritual which he does not reveal. When undisciplined beings attempt to work the Great Work ... we are witness to the results. A lack of vetting (especially genetic) disturbed this operation since its commencement. Our complacent satisfaction over the stupendous bravery of Captain Rice volunteering for such a profound and absurd mission—we knew that he would volunteer—led us to push the initiation ... led me to rush a man and a woman's existence into the unknown, into their existence. That accounts for much of the eclecticism you have seen in his report, if there really is any. The species has probably become more clear to your Excellency in any case.

I am not advocating a rescue mission for either of them, Rice or Elioud, on this stage. Nor am I advocating an interactive mentorship with them, such as we had with our ambassadors during their present Dome's construction. I have seen that it would be resented. Just as we have seen that our distance is resented. Complex and curious they are, your Excellency. So many details about them are necessarily overlooked by a third party. Nonetheless I suggest a new policy of disinterested encouragement. We will still keep our protective watch radiating from our more subtle wagons that whip through their atmosphere tracing arcane patterns of alert. But they alone must learn to tame their strange compositions with those famished twin'd gods whom they are now free to face in a naked world. This is Venus's legacy and it was his personal complaint—let his species inherit it. A confident and reflective soul must develop somewhere among them if they are to warrant our further attentions. From a body which they must regard as sacred—to us, mere manure—a diamond flower may be coaxed to grow. A difficult process, and we may wonder whom it will please most, as we dispatch with a platinum lance—our choice weapon!—yet another onslaught of the Enemy's minions who wrongly interpret our inquiry into the structure of life as an opportunity for a cowardly ambush; they are sorry for their haste now; they are spitted and blown away back to the void-bound dust of a soul-less fate ...

If you approve it, my recommended strategy should also bring us that much closer to our own object in this dimension of the Multiverse's most consummate potential for self-reflection and love's manifestation, that of the Human species; it is the same as theirs. A new work for the mortal empire. Yes, rereading through the last paragraphs of his report confirms this idea. As he said in the beginning, 'it is evidenced'.—Major Bunder, Cosmic Ranger, 7ᵗʰ Legion]

www.ingramcontent.com/pod-product-compliance
Lightning Source LLC
Chambersburg PA
CBHW030334030726
47499CB00003B/768